THE ZEBRA WALL

BOOKS BY KEVIN HENKES

All Alone

Clean Enough

Margaret & Taylor

Return to Sender

Bailey Goes Camping

Grandpa & Bo

A Weekend with Wendell

Once Around the Block
(illustrated by Victoria Chess)

Two Under Par

Sheila Rae, the Brave

The Zebra Wall

THE ZEBRA WALL

by Kevin Henkes

Greenwillow Books New York

First Edition   1 2 3 4 5 6 7 8 9 10

Library of Congress Cataloging-in-Publication Data
Henkes, Kevin.
The zebra wall / by Kevin Henkes.
p.   cm.
Summary: When ten-year-old Adine's mother has a new baby,
eccentric Aunt Irene comes to stay and shares Adine's bedroom
—an event which requires a great deal of adjustment.
ISBN 0-688-07568-1 (lib. bdg.)
[1. Aunts—Fiction. 2. Babies—Fiction.
3. Family life—Fiction.]   I. Title
PZ7.H389Ze 1988 [Fic]—dc19 87-18454 CIP AC

For Laura

Contents

THE ZEBRA WALL

1

Spaghetti Sauce

The long list of names was fastened to the refrigerator door with a thick, hot pink magnet in the shape of an ice-cream cone. At the top of the list was the name Francine, at the bottom—Frito. In between was everything from Faye to Florence.

The list on the refrigerator was a sampling of potential names for the new Vorlob baby.

There were no boys' names on the list because the Vorlobs were certain that the baby would be a girl. They were positive. And why wouldn't they be? There were five girls in the Vorlob family already—Adine (age ten), Bernice (age eight), Carla (age seven), Dot (age four), and Effie (age two). It just seemed fitting and logical that the new baby would be a girl and that her name should begin with the letter *F*.

Everyone in the family could add as many names to the list as they wanted. Then, after the baby was born—and everyone had had a good look at her—they would have a family meeting and vote.

Adine had written only one name on the list—Florinda. She hoped that everyone would vote for Florinda, but she had her doubts. Bernice and Carla were both pulling for Francine, Dot couldn't decide between Flopsy ("After Peter Rabbit's sister!" she'd yell), and Frito ("After my favorite food!" she'd squeal), and

Effie was too little to understand. Mr. Vorlob just kept adding names to the list without voicing his opinion. And Mrs. Vorlob kept saying, "I've always loved the name Phyllis—it's so classy—but I doubt if I'll ever make it to the letter *P*. Maybe we could spell it with an *F*."

Adine thought that Phyllis—spelled with an *F* or a *P*, or spelled *backward*, for that matter—was anything but classy. In fact, Adine wasn't too fond of any of their names, including her own. Adine. *Especially* her own. She preferred names like Melissa and Jennifer Rose and Courtney and Heather. When she recently told her mother about this, Mrs. Vorlob said, "Adine, those are such fancy-shmancy names. You and your sisters' names have class, and they're earthy. Sturdy as rock."

I'd rather not be compared to a rock, Adine felt like saying. But she didn't. She knew it wasn't worth getting into. If her mother had her mind set a certain way, Adine doubted if even a Mack truck could budge it.

Determined, was how Mr. Vorlob described his wife. Adine thought that stubborn was a more fitting word. "At least you always know where you stand with me," Adine heard her mother say on the phone once, in her thick, burly voice. "I don't pussyfoot around. And I'm not like some people who let things bottle up inside them."

Adine was like that. She'd keep things to herself until her stomach felt like a Sunbeam blender on high speed. And that's exactly how she felt right now. She had found out earlier that morning that she would have to share her bedroom with her Aunt Irene. Aunt Irene would be coming to help out with the new baby.

"How long is Aunt Irene staying?" Adine asked her mother, twisting a strand of her hair around and around her finger. Adine's hair was straight, nearly white, and hung down past her waist. Mrs. Vorlob was sitting at the kitchen table, waiting for the large pot of spaghetti sauce on the counter to cool. She was going to pour the sauce into her Tupperware containers to freeze for Mr. Vorlob to heat up when she was in the hospital. And for when she came home afterward and wouldn't feel like cooking.

"She'll stay until I get back on my feet after the baby," Mrs. Vorlob replied, a carrot stick dangling out of the corner of her mouth. She was substituting carrot and celery sticks for cigarettes while she was pregnant. She even filled her leather cigarette case with them to bring along if she and Mr. Vorlob happened to be going out. In imitation, Carla and Dot had taken up pretend-smoking with vegetables, too, which Adine thought looked silly.

"How long will that be?" Adine pressed.

"I don't know, Adine," Mrs. Vorlob answered, flicking the carrot stick over an empty ashtray and blowing imaginary smoke. "A week, a month. However long it takes." She took a bite of the carrot, crunching it loudly as she chewed. Mrs. Vorlob was wearing her bright yellow, terry maternity dress. Her short blond hair ended midway down her neck and seemed to melt into the color of the dress. Adine thought that her mother looked pretty in the dress. Adine also thought that her mother looked like a giant pear. Thick and round and swelling.

"I can help out all you need," Adine offered. "I really will."

"I know that, honey," Mrs. Vorlob said, smiling. "You're my biggest helper around the house. But it'll just be nice for me to have my sister here. Understand?"

Adine shrugged.

"I know you don't want Irene to come, but she *is* my sister. And she's been having a hard time since her divorce. It'll be good for her to be surrounded by family—day and night—for a while." Mrs. Vorlob took a long breath and placed her hands on her abdomen. "I know deep down you understand."

"Okay, Mom," Adine said. "I understand."

And she did. Sort of. Adine understood that Aunt Irene was coming and that there was nothing she could do about it. Nothing at all.

"Anyway, Adine, it's more than a month away," Mrs. Vorlob said cheerfully. "Put it out of your mind for now."

Adine wanted to be mad at her mother, but she wouldn't let herself. After all, Mrs. Vorlob always seemed to come through for Adine when she needed it most. And Adine could tell her mother things that she wouldn't think of telling anyone else. Private things that often hurt. Like last school year, when Mr. and Mrs. Vorlob came to Adine's class for Parents' Day wearing blue jeans, plaid flannel shirts, and their matching, sateen Milwaukee Brewers jackets. Mr. Vorlob's hair was the exact shade and length of his wife's. And their husky bodies looked like carbon copies. All of which caused Adine's classmate, Gary Wilker, to say, "Adine, I can't tell your mom and dad apart.

They look like twins. Short, fat, men twins. They're identical." Then he laughed.

Adine held out all day, but burst into tears upon arriving home. She reluctantly told her mother about Gary Wilker.

"Oh, Adine," Mrs. Vorlob said, hugging her. "Don't worry about it. I'm not going to let something like that ruin my day, and you shouldn't, either. I wouldn't put much stock in Mr. Gary Wilker. Isn't he the one who flung tabs of butter around the cafeteria when I had lunch supervision?"

Adine nodded. She couldn't understand how her mother could be so calm. She also couldn't understand why her mother wore blue jeans, plaid flannel shirts, and her Brewers jacket all the time. "Couldn't you wear dresses more often or let your hair grow?"

"Adine," her mother said, lighting a cigarette, "I don't *like* dresses—unless I'm pregnant. And I don't like long hair on me. *And*, I'm not going to change for Gary Wilker."

What about changing for me? Adine said to herself, watching smoke stream out from between her mother's plump lips.

"I'll tell you what, though," Mrs. Vorlob said. "I guarantee you I'll come up with something."

And she did. The very next morning Mr. Vorlob stopped shaving. Soon he had a thick, golden beard that curled like pencil shavings around his face. And Mrs. Vorlob started wearing her hair a *bit* longer. She let it fall a couple of inches over her shirt collars before she got it cut now. "I don't think that even Gary Wilker would confuse us now," Mrs. Vorlob whispered to Adine one night, winking.

It was because of things like that, that Adine had a hard time harboring a grudge against her mother. Even if Aunt Irene *was* coming.

Mrs. Vorlob rose from the kitchen table, holding a celery stick between her forefinger and thumb, her other fingers spread out like a fan. "Well, ready or not, I'm going to freeze the sauce," she said. "I want to get this done before your dad and your sisters come home from the hardware store, or there'll be spaghetti sauce everywhere but in the freezer. Want to help?"

"Sure," Adine replied.

"I hope the hardware store has the right colors of paint so we can finish the nursery."

"We could paint tonight," Adine suggested. "It'd be fun."

"Oooooh," Mrs. Vorlob said suddenly, dropping the celery stick into the pot of sauce, then laughing. "Phyllis with an *F* is dancing, I think. A fast dance. I wouldn't be surprised if she was singing, too. Want to listen?"

Adine rested her head against her mother. "I hear her," she said. Then, very softly, she whispered into her mother's dress, "Hello, Florinda, this is your sister, Adine."

2

The *F* Wall

By the time Adine's father and sisters returned
from the hardware store, the spaghetti sauce
was in the freezer and Adine and her mother
were waiting on the front porch with Mrs.
Vorlob's packed suitcase. Mrs. Vorlob was leaning against the door, cradling her belly. Adine
was perched atop the railing, like a squirrel on a
branch.

Bernice, Carla, and Dot raced up the side-walk, each carrying a small can of paint. Effie dawdled behind, clutching a large, flat paint-brush and sucking on it. Mr. Vorlob brought up the rear, swinging a gallon of Colonial White, a silver prize at the end of his solid arm. Bullets of sunlight ricocheted off the large can of paint. "We got all the colors, Helen!" Mr. Vorlob yelled.

"Roland, it's time," Mrs. Vorlob said calmly, when he reached the porch. "Let's go to the hospital."

"*Already?*" Mr. Vorlob asked, setting the paint near the front door. "You're not due for a month."

"Mama's like a library book—due in a month, due in a month," Dot said in a singsong voice.

"It's time," Mrs. Vorlob repeated. "I know it's time." She turned to face her daughters and grimaced. "Girls, Adine's in charge until Aunt Irene arrives. I called her on the phone; she'll be here any minute. Now, mind Adine and give me a quick kiss. And by the time I come home with your new baby sister, I want the nursery wall finished. Do a good job and make me proud. You know how much that means to me."

Mr. Vorlob blew a kiss in the general direction of his daughters and helped his wife into their converted school bus (the only lime-green bus in Mason, Wisconsin). "Be good," he called. "I'll give you a jingle from the hospital," he added, before pulling out into the street and rumbling away.

Adine picked up the gallon of paint; it hit her bare leg and she was sure it would bruise. When Adine was younger, her father called her "Miss Banana," she bruised so easily. And in third grade, when Adine's class was learning about similies and metaphors, Mary Rose Wampole said, "Adine Vorlob's skin's as white as my mother's new Kenmore washer." From that day on, Adine wasn't terribly fond of Mary Rose Wampole.

"Come on, you guys," Adine said to her sisters. "Let's go paint. Let's paint the wall for Mom."

"I get to use the little brush," Bernice said, running into the house.

"*I* do!" Carla shouted after her.

"I get the new, fat brush," Dot announced, grabbing the brush out of Effie's dimpled fingers.

Effie started to cry. "Where's Mama? I want Mama!"

"It's okay, Ef," Adine soothed, starting to cry herself. She took Effie by the hand and pulled her into the house behind her. "Mama's gonna come home soon with a new baby sister for us. You just wait and see."

The blender inside Adine was revving up again; she was worried about her mother.

The nursery was nearly completed. The same crib that had been Adine's stood in the

center of the room beneath a mobile Mr.
Vorlob had made from a mail-order kit. The
mobile consisted of seven little fawns hanging
down with cord at various lengths from a wire
framework. Mr. Vorlob had painted a tiny letter *F* on each of the fawn's chests. The small,
white dresser, which had also been Adine's,
stood nearby. Mrs. Vorlob had stenciled bright
*F*s up and down its sides and across all the
drawers just a week earlier.When Adine had
been born, the dresser was decorated with *A*s;
it was repainted when each of Adine's sisters
was born—with *B*s for Bernice, *C*s for Carla,
*D*s for Dot, and *E*s for Effie.

Three of the walls in the nursery were
painted a color called fuchsia. Originally, the
color had been so bright that Mr. Vorlob had
added brown and black paint to it to tone it
down. The resulting color reminded Adine of
liver before her mother fried it. Adine thought
the color looked as bad as liver tasted. When
Adine expressed her dislike of the dark purplish

red, Mrs. Vorlob explained, "But, honey, it's the only color we could find that began with *F*. And I really want to keep things coordinated. It'll grow on you."

The other wall was only half finished. It was the focal point of the room. It was the wall you faced when you entered the room. No windows or doors interrupted it. It was Mrs. Vorlob's pride and joy.

The wall was a mural—a mural of things that began with the letter *F*. Mr. and Mrs. Vorlob had drawn the mural using pictures from their daughters' coloring books as patterns. The entire family got to help paint it. Dot, and especially Effie (who usually settled for painting on newspaper), needed close supervision, but everyone worked together, filling in the penciled outlines with thick, vivid colors. Kind of like a paint-by-number, Adine thought. They had been working on the mural nearly every night after dinner, until the evening they had run out of certain shades and were so low on Colonial White (which Mr. and Mrs. Vorlob used for mixing lighter hues) that they had to stop temporarily.

The Vorlobs referred to the mural as "the *F* wall." There were flowers and frogs and a fox on the wall. There were fish and ferns and a farm. On the upper left-hand corner of the wall was a fairy with silvery wings. The fairy held a wand that pointed to the words: THIS WALL BE-LONGS TO. There was a blank space after the words. "We'll fill in the blank with the baby's name after she's home and we've decided what to call her," Mrs. Vorlob had said. Adine loved the way the fairy's wings shimmered when the sun fell upon them in the early morning, but her favorite part of the wall was a large star her father had painted. The star was metallic gold and it had a wavy tail that streaked across the entire mural like the ruffled path a boat makes in water. The tail changed from gold to silver to yellow to orange to pink. When Adine's mother first saw the star she was upset. "Oh, Roland!"

she said testily. "How could you put a shooting star on our *F* wall?"

"It's not a *shooting* star, Helen," he explained patiently. "It's a *falling* star. Relax."

It occurred to Adine how important the *F* wall was to her mother, when Adine found her alone one afternoon sitting cross-legged in the nursery, staring at the half-completed mural.

"When we finish the *F* wall," Mrs. Vorlob said, "I'm thinking of sending a photo of it to one of those ladies' magazines your Aunt Irene always buys. Who knows—it might get in."

Adine remembered the look on her mother's face that day. Dreamy. Dreamy and far away. Adine had never seen her mother look that way before. Ever.

"I might send in photos of the murals we did when you and your sisters were babies, too," Mrs. Vorlob went on. "Maybe they'd do a whole feature on us."

Of course Adine couldn't remember what the mural in her own nursery had actually looked like, but photos of the wall showed apples and angels and apricots. An airplane. A map of Africa. A pirouetting alligator wearing a frilly tutu. A long line of ants spelled out the words THIS WALL BELONGS TO ADINE. Trailing after the ants was a fat anteater, appearing hungry and somewhat goofy with eyes bulging out of his head like peas popping out of pods. Adine had seen the photos so many times that she had a perfect picture of the wall in her mind's eye.

Adine stared at the *F* wall (not unlike her mother had done), until the images of the fairy and the falling star blurred and blended into one another. Bits of wing and color swirling like oil in a puddle. Around and around.

"Adine!" someone shouted. "Adine!" It was Bernice. She and Carla had tried to open the new can of Colonial White. They had succeeded. But, in the process, they had also succeeded in tipping it over. A miniature ocean of paint was spreading across the floor.

"Oh, no!" Adine cried desperately. She

tugged at her right ear, as she often did when she felt completely helpless. "Oh, no!" Upset and confused, Adine stood paralyzed as the paint oozed toward her. She blinked and a tear rolled down her cheek.

"Let's not tug at our ears—there's work to be done here," a booming voice said from the hallway, startling all five Vorlob sisters. "Get the lead out, ladies!"

Aunt Irene had arrived.

3

Aunt Irene

Aunt Irene was hard to figure out. She was older—probably fifty—but she was still energetic and curious. Things Adine thought you lost as you grew older. Aunt Irene was gruff and large and loud and strong, and yet Adine had seen her cry endlessly, watching TV movies, and get weepy at the sight of a clumsy puppy. Spots, connected by knobby blue veins, covered her leathery hands, but her nails were always remarkably beautiful—as pink and lustrous as seashells, as if she worked on them for hours each day.

When Aunt Irene visited, Adine always tried to hide until the welcoming hugs and kisses were over. Getting hugged by Aunt Irene was like getting tackled by a football player. The fleshy undersides of her arms reminded Adine of lumpy mashed potatoes, but they were extremely powerful. If, for some reason, she didn't hug you, she'd thwack you on the back, which was worse. And her kisses were sharp. Sharp, because she had a slight, but prickly, mustache and stale, gamy breath.

Aunt Irene smoked thin, brown cigarettes, which Adine hated more than the regular cigarettes her mother smoked. And she frequently made whistling noises when the exhaling smoke poured out of her nostrils. "I'm a steam engine," she'd say in a deep freight-train voice as she chugged about in circles, to Dot and Effie's delight. She'd always come to a screeching halt by taking out her teeth and hissing. Adine thought it was disgusting. But the worst thing about Aunt Irene was her cats. She had a real one—gray with black splotches, named Deedee—that came with her wherever she went. And she had more than two thousand other ones that she collected. They filled her house and covered her body.

Aunt Irene owned cat bookends, cat curtains, a cat toilet-seat cover, cat rugs, and cat mugs. Bed sheets with cats, dishes with cats, and pillows with cats embroidered on in gaudy thread. Stuffed cats, porcelain cats, wooden cats. Cats painted on black velvet and framed in chrome hung on her living-room walls. And a set of cat pot holders hung from hooks in her kitchen. Many of Aunt Irene's clothes had cats printed on them, too—blouses, skirts, scarves. She always carried her wicker cat purse and wore one of her numerous pairs of cat earrings. And a tiny gold cat was even stamped on the lower corner of one of her enormous eyeglass lenses.

For Mrs. Vorlob's sake, Adine always politely tolerated her eccentric aunt. She even found her amusing on occasion. But that was before Adine suffered public harassment and private humiliation on account of Aunt Irene.

A few months earlier, Aunt Irene had been featured in the *Mason Journal Times*'s "Cook of the Week" column. Beneath a large photo of the cook in her kitchen were printed her recipes for Cowboy Pudding (Spanish Rice), Cornflake Balls, and Chocolate Oil Cake, complete with suggestions for frosting and little cat garnishes made from chocolate wafers and licorice. That part was okay. The bad part was the photo. Aunt Irene had been captured in an awkward pose. One eye closed. Nostrils flared. She was pretending to be mixing batter in her largest cat bowl, one of her cigarettes hanging out of her mouth like an oversized cocktail toothpick. Cats were everywhere. On her apron, on the tablecloth, on the dishrag draped over her elbow. Deedee was on her shoulders. And a stuffed Sylvester from Six Flags Great America was propped up on one of the kitchen chairs, its head resting on the tabletop.

Adine blushed as she'd stared at the newspaper. What an embarrassment! Adine was glad that her aunt's last name was Glickman. Maybe no one would know she was related. And then Adine read the accompanying article. She could have died right then and there.

After discussing her cats, Aunt Irene stated that her recipes were "surefire pleasers." She said that her Cornflake Balls were her niece Adine's favorite. Adine blinked her eyes, but her name didn't disappear. She didn't think anyone else on earth was named Adine. At least not in Mason, Wisconsin. Now everyone would know that the crazy cat-lady was her aunt. Adine had dreaded going to school the next day.

The next morning, Adine spotted Gary

Wilker waiting by the chain-link fence that bordered the playground at school. When she was within hearing range, he squinted, twisted his face, and began meowing in a whiny voice. By the afternoon recess he had talked Mary Rose Wampole, Dirk Reese, and Chad Biddle into joining him.

"Do you want me to call Gary Wilker's mother?" Mrs. Vorlob asked, when Adine told her what had happened. "I'd love to set her straight, but knowing me, it just might make things worse."

Adine agreed to leaving her mother out of it.

"Oh, hon," Mrs. Vorlob said, "just bark at them if they do it tomorrow. Bark like a German Shepherd and scare their pants off."

After pecking Adine on the top of her head, Mrs. Vorlob took the clipping of Aunt Irene down from its place of honor on the refrigerator door and placed it inside the phone book, hiding it deep within the thickness of names and numbers.

When Gary Wilker met Adine the following school day, hunched and sounding like a stray cat in a fight, Adine sucked in her breath, clenched her fists at her sides, and then barked as loudly and fiercely as she could. Gary Wilker's mouth dropped and froze. He stood motionless, as if tempting Adine to continue. As the first bell rang, Adine focused on his shin, closed her eyes again, and kicked him with all her might. Flushed, Adine ran up the worn stone steps two at a time, without looking back. She vowed she'd never eat another Cornflake Ball again. And even though she knew it really wasn't Aunt Irene's fault, Adine was certain she'd never forgive her. How could she?

And there was the special May Day cake, too. Maybe that was worst of all. It had been Adine's first cake made from scratch without supervision (except that Mrs. Vorlob had taken the pans from the oven and released the cakes from the pans when they had cooled). And it had been lovely. Two round, golden pillows (only slightly uneven), with instant vanilla pudding in between. Pale pink frosting sprinkled with coconut flakes topped it off, like snow on a bed of apple blossoms. It sat on the kitchen table, just waiting while the Vorlobs and Aunt Irene ate dinner in the dining room. Adine pushed her chipped beef and parsley-buttered potatoes around her plate, anxious to present her masterpiece. When the time finally came and Adine rushed into the kitchen, she found Deedee on the tabletop, masked in pink frosting, surrounded by yellow crumbs. Deedee had ruined Adine's cake, turning it into a jumbled mess.

Adine went weak. "Help!" she called.

Everyone ran to the kitchen.

Aunt Irene thought it was hilarious. "I'm so sorry, sweets, but you can always bake another cake," she said as she snapped photos of Deedee, with Mr. Vorlob's Polaroid. "But I might *never* get another chance at photos like these! They're adorable!"

Mr. and Mrs. Vorlob tried to salvage the cake and quiet Aunt Irene. "It's a terrific cake, Adine," said her father. "A beaut," said her mother. But all their praise fell flat when Adine looked at the lopsided mound.

"I'm not gonna *eat* it!" screamed Carla in the background. "It's got *cat* germs!"

Adine replayed the scene in her head so many times that it remained as vivid as on the day it actually had happened.

In Adine's opinion, Aunt Irene had a lot of reconciling to do. Adine figured that considering her aunt's age, she'd most likely be dead before she even came close to making up for the bad things she and Deedee had caused.

"Isn't it nice to have things under control?" asked Aunt Irene, after the floor in the nursery had been wiped up. Before anyone could respond, she answered herself, "Yes. It surely is." Aunt Irene rubbed her hands together as she talked, causing the heavy charm bracelets that dangled from her wrists to jingle. Deedee had had one litter of kittens before she was spayed; there was one silver charm representing each of them on either bracelet, plus one for each of Deedee's "grandkitties." The charms currently numbered twenty-eight. The bracelets looked uncomfortable to Adine, and she wondered how long Aunt Irene would continue to add charms. She pictured her aunt with a spangled network of charms laced around her neck and waist and ankles like prison chains.

They were all seated at the kitchen table, fixing bologna-and-cheese sandwiches. It was June. The windows were open and the summer breeze swept through the room, making the curtains billow. Aunt Irene had brought out Mrs. Vorlob's cookie cutters from the pantry. "You can make darling sandwiches with these, girls," she said. "Watch." Aunt Irene cut like a machine. She slapped cheese hearts and stars on bologna, and bologna rabbits and flowers on slices of cheese. Bernice, Carla, Dot, and Effie were thrilled. They cut out more shapes and decorated their sandwiches with ketchup, mustard, and pickle relish. Eating became a game and they enjoyed themselves.

Adine made herself a regular sandwich. She was in no mood to have fun. Her sisters' laughter annoyed her. After all, their mother was in the hospital. Maybe having a baby right then. And she wasn't due for a month. Adine took tiny bites. She peevishly played with her crusts. She scowled at Deedee.

Deedee was slumped across Aunt Irene's shoulders, her tail coiled around Aunt Irene's neck. Adine itched just looking at her. She wasn't allergic, but she could have been, Deedee affected her so. When Adine thought no one was watching, she stuck her tongue out at Deedee. Deedee bared her teeth, then chattered, her rhinestone collar gleaming.

"Adine, you don't have to be so quiet," Aunt Irene said, holding up a thin strip of bologna, which Deedee devoured instantly. "Neither Deedee nor I bite."

Adine's face grew hot. "I know," she whispered uneasily. She wasn't sure about Deedee, though.

Effie giggled. "*I* bite!" she shouted. She began chomping loudly on her sandwich to prove her point. She kicked her feet and her high chair hopped.

Aunt Irene ate greedily. Three sandwiches. While she chewed, her arms circled her plate like a frame around a painting, guarding her lunch. And then, when they were putting the food away and cleaning off the table, she rolled up a piece of bologna and stuffed it into her mouth.

"Dad says we can't have lunch meat without bread," Adine said quietly and carefully. "It's wasteful."

Aunt Irene swallowed hard. "The damage is done, sweetie," she said, wiping her mouth with the back of her hand. She burped and excused herself. "Girls," she told Bernice, Carla, Dot, and Effie, "go brush your teeth. I want a few minutes with Adine." When they were alone, Aunt Irene asked Adine, "What is it with us? Whenever I see you it's like starting all over again. Hurry up and warm up to me. Even if it's just a teensy bit."

Adine broke into tears and started walking away. Aunt Irene swung around and grabbed Adine, pressing her close to her ample bosom.

"There, there," Aunt Irene said. "I'm so sorry, sweetie. Is it your crazy aunt who's upset you, or is it your mother?"

Adine nodded. She *was* thinking about her mother. But she was also thinking about Cornflake Balls and the May Day cake.

"Now, don't worry about your mother. Next to me, she's the toughest person I know. And when it comes to babies, Helen Vorlob's *the* expert." Aunt Irene reached under the cuff of her sleeve and pulled out a tissue. "Here, sweetie— clean it out," she said. She whisked Adine's hair away from her eyes. "While we wait for your dad to call, let's go finish that wall for your mother. If we work hard, we can take a break at four o'clock to watch 'Lifestyles of the Rich and Famous.'" She smiled broadly. "What do you say?"

"Okay," Adine squeaked.

Aunt Irene brushed some crumbs off her Felix the Cat sweatshirt and led the way to the nursery, her feet clomping like anvils. Deedee was at her heels. And Adine was close behind.

4

The Phone Call

"Organization is the key," Aunt Irene repeated again and again, as she lined a row of Styrofoam cups along the *F* wall. The cups were filled with the different shades of paint that she had just mixed. The colors looked beautiful, inviting. Adine was tempted to stick her fingers into every cup. But she didn't dare, with Aunt Irene around.

Carla was so eager to begin, she grabbed for the cup containing light purple paint. "Let's start!" she shrieked.

Aunt Irene slid the paint out of her reach. "Patience is a virtue," she said.

"Okay, Auntie," Carla said, backing away.

"Patience is a choo-choo," Dot began singing in her shrill little voice. "Choo-choo. Choo-choo."

Adine only hoped that Aunt Irene wouldn't light one of her brown cigarettes and do *her* impersonation of a train. Dot's was bad enough.

"Aunt Irene, you'd be good in the army," Bernice said, giggling. "Daddy even said so."

Aunt Irene didn't seem thrilled by the comment, but she didn't seem offended by it, either. It occurred to Adine that Aunt Irene *would* be good in the army. Maybe that was why Uncle Gilly had left her and moved to Iowa. If Adine was stuck in a small apartment crammed with Aunt Irene and thousands of cats, she'd take off, too. No doubt about it.

Since her divorce, Aunt Irene had been coming over to the Vorlobs' more often and staying later. And now, with such a good excuse—helping out while Mrs. Vorlob was in the hospital and after the new baby arrived—Adine wondered if she'd ever leave.

Aunt Irene finally granted permission, and the painting began in earnest. The sisters were shoulder to shoulder, facing the wall (except for Effie, who was napping in her undersized trundle bed with guardrails, which had been rolled into the nursery). Adine worked quietly, squatting low, using green paint to make spots on the back of a frog near the bottom of the wall. The top part of the mural was completed, so no ladder was needed. Aunt Irene paced back and forth behind them, stroking Deedee and puffing methodically on one of her cigarettes.

"Aren't you going to paint, Auntie?" asked Carla. "You just have to fill in the lines."

"Yeah," said Bernice. "It's just like doing a coloring book."

"My coloring book is almost filled," Dot told Aunt Irene, airily. "And when I'm *all* done, Mama says I can get a *new* one!"

"The only reason you finish your books so fast is because you color all over the page," Carla said. Then she turned toward Aunt Irene and whispered ferociously, "She can't stay in the lines at all."

"Yes, I can!" Dot exclaimed. "I can, too! Too-too-too!" Soon Dot's "too-too-too"s turned into "choo-choo-choo"s, and then she begged Aunt Irene to do her steam-engine impression. "Do it, do it, do it!" she pleaded. *"Please!"*

Aunt Irene obliged. Surprisingly, Effie remained asleep, twisting and turning as if a real train passed in a dream.

Aunt Irene coughed. "Enough for now," she said. "I usually don't inhale so much," she explained, coughing some more. She picked up a brush. "Maybe I *will* try painting."

They painted for nearly an hour. And then, instead of continuing to simply fill in the predrawn lines, Aunt Irene painted a black-and-gray cat on the bottom of the mural, right above the baseboard.

Adine was the first to notice it, but Bernice was the first to say something. "Aunt Irene?" she said. "This is our *F* wall. Cat begins with a *C*."

"Cat is C-A-T," Carla chimed in.

"Maybe it's supposed to be Deedee!" Dot said.

Carla spelled in the air with her paint-speckled finger. "But Deedee begins with a *D.*"

"All I know," Adine said, "is that Mom'll be upset."

Aunt Irene sighed. "Dear nieces—it's a fe-line. F-E-L-I-N-E. Don't worry, your mother will love it. Trust me."

"Maybe we should name the baby Feline," Carla said. "I like it better than Francine."

Adine groaned. She was still hoping to name the baby Florinda.

"I checked out your list of names," Aunt

Irene said. "I'd vote for Flo. Maybe the baby
would grow up to be like Flo on 'Alice,' the TV
show. She's spunky and whippy and indepen-
dent. She always gets good dates, too. I watch
the reruns every night after the news, unless
there's a John Wayne movie on." Aunt Irene
laughed. "I wish *I'd* get good dates."

Adine was glad that Aunt Irene didn't get to
vote on the baby's name. She thought Flo was a
horrible name. Almost as bad as Adine. When
she was old enough, Adine was going to change
her name. Change it to Angelique. That way,
she'd have a beautiful name and her mother
would still have all her children's names corre-
spond with the alphabet. Adine didn't understand her mother's alphabetical naming one bit.
It seemed to Adine that if a baby looked like a
Veronica or a Gloria or a William, you should
just name him or her accordingly and not
worry about what letter his or her name began
with.

Earlier that summer, at Girl Scout day camp,

Adine had to pick a nickname for herself; all the campers had to. She'd chosen Angelique, looking forward to a week of being called the name she secretly loved. But Mrs. Schliesman, the troop leader, made her choose a different nickname. "Let's be creative, Adine. Anyone can be named Angelique. How about something more original? How about Polliwog?" Adine winced, but agreed to it. And so, for an unbearable week, Adine was known as Polliwog. The memory made her shudder.

The phone rang and Adine instantly forgot about day camp. Everyone jumped. Deedee, who had been in the crib batting at the fawn mobile, suddenly leapt out and darted through the doorway toward the ringing.

Aunt Irene answered. "Hello?"

The girls gathered around her. Adine's entire body was shaking, her heart racing.

"Yes . . . yes . . . yes . . .," Aunt Irene said. "You're kidding? . . . And Helen? . . . You're

sure? . . . *Positive?* . . . Thank goodness! . . .
Oh, good. . . . Well, it could be worse. . . . I'll
be waiting, Roland. . . . Yes, the girls are
fine. . . . I'll tell them. . . . Oh, and Roland, I
didn't think you had it in you," she joked in
closing.

"Well, girls," Aunt Irene said solemnly, holding the receiver against her chest. "There's good
news, bad news, and a surprise. The good
news is that there's a new Vorlob baby and that
your mother's doing fine. Absolutely fine."

Adine sighed in relief.

Aunt Irene hung up the phone and continued. "The bad news is that the baby was, of
course, a bit premature—just a button of a
thing. Four pounds and six ounces. But your
father says everything will be okay. The baby's
got some of *my* blood, so I'm sure it's a fighter."
Aunt Irene cleared her throat and paused. An
impressive pause. She got dramatic with her
hands. "*And*, the surprise is . . . the baby's a
boy!"

Adine, Bernice, Carla, and Dot could barely believe it. A *boy*. They didn't know what to think. What do you do with a baby brother? Instinctively, they began screaming and hopping and hugging. Effie, still hazy from her nap, padded into the kitchen and slowly joined in the joyful ruckus. They held hands and circled around Aunt Irene as if she were a maypole.

"We have to celebrate," said Aunt Irene. "I'll treat you to McDonald's for dinner."

A boy, thought Adine. A real, live baby boy!

5

Night

Adine had a difficult time sleeping. Partially due to the excitement about her new brother. Partially due to Aunt Irene's continuous snoring. Partially due to Deedee, who periodically charged around the room as if her tail were on fire. And partially because Adine had to sleep on a thin, scratchy cot, while Aunt Irene dreamed in Adine's spongy bed.

Night

The darkness was velvety, and Adine pawed at the air as if it could be touched. What a day it had been, she thought, drawing a skinny little baby in the blackness with her finger. Babies weren't out of the ordinary in the Vorlob house. Baby girls, that is. A baby boy was another story.

Adine had grown used to the usual baby preparations—redecorating the nursery furniture, painting the mural, the list of names. It was kind of like getting ready for Christmas; there were a number of things to do, but it basically stayed the same, time after time. But now things were different. Adine had a brother. A *brother*. Would his name begin with an *F*? Or would her parents want to start all over with an *A* because he was the first boy? If that's what they decided to do, they'd have to repaint the mural.

Deedee pounced on Adine's stomach, then zipped off toward the closet. Adine sat up in the cot. "Stupid cat," she whispered. More than anything, Adine wanted to make sure that the baby was healthy. Her mother, too. Nothing like this had ever happened before. Her worrying was what was really keeping her awake. Tears sneaked out of the corners of her eyes.

I wonder if something's wrong with me? Adine asked herself. None of her sisters seemed upset about the baby. And even Effie seemed to be getting along fine without Mrs. Vorlob. Adine heard Deedee kneading the throw rug, her claws pulling on the threads and snapping them. Deedee's lucky, Adine thought. It must be easy to be a cat. They've nothing to worry about.

Adine carefully rose from the cot and groped through the darkness toward the bedroom door. She tripped over something—maybe a shoe—and quietly caught herself from falling by grabbing onto her dresser. With arms outstretched, she found the wall and slowly followed it to the doorframe. She tiptoed to her parents' room.

Adine glanced out the wide hall window on

her way and checked the night sky. It was clear. The stars were like diamonds scattered across an expanse of black velour. "Good," she whispered. There was one thing Adine disliked as much as her name and Aunt Irene. Storms. In fact, she was afraid of them. Especially the kind that sprang up unannounced after everyone was asleep. They paralyzed her with their thunder and lightning and wind. She knew she was too old to fear them, but how can you help the way you feel at the bottom of your stomach? A summer storm is the last thing I need tonight, Adine thought, as she gingerly opened the door to her parents' room.

The room was empty, the bed made. Adine pulled the spread and the blankets back and climbed under them, sinking into the bed like syrup. She loved the spread on her parents' bed. It was the color of tea with milk, patterned with bursting, deep gold chrysanthemums. The chrysanthemums reminded Adine of the way she used to paint pictures of the sun when she was younger—large, curvy watercolor shapes that frayed out at the edges in lacy filaments. Yellow fireworks.

Adine sniffed the sheets and pillows. She could detect traces of both her parents. Her mother's was the light soapy scent (because she hadn't been smoking); her father's was the earthy one, like newly mown grass. Adine buried her face beneath the mound of pillows and fell asleep.

Earlier that evening, when Mr. Vorlob briefly stopped by the house, he appeared worried to Adine. But he repeatedly exclaimed, "Can you believe it?! A boy!" And he smoked (and chewed on) two fat, self-congratulatory cigars. One right after the other. Aunt Irene smoked one, too.

Adine and her sisters asked a legion of questions about their new brother and about their mother. Mr. Vorlob assured them that both mother and son were doing fine. The girls surrounded him on the sofa like petals on a flower, drawing close when he described their brother. "I can tell he's going to be plucky, despite his size," Mr. Vorlob said, holding out his hands to indicate the baby's length. "Like I told you, he's tiny, but the fierce way he points his little red toes and cocks his shriveled fists makes him look like he's ready for a fight." Mr. Vorlob toyed with his cigar butt and chuckled. "Your brother's a character, all right. You know, I keep picturing him wearing boxing gloves, his delicate body jumping up and down in the hospital crib as if it were a boxing ring. Shoot." Mr. Vorlob threw a playful jab at each of his daughters.

"Is he littler than I was?" Dot asked.

"And me?" Carla added.

"Dot and Carla, you two were horses in comparison. That little guy is the tiniest baby I've ever seen. The nurses even put a blue knitted cap on his head, to keep his body heat in. Your mama says he reminds her of a robin's egg—

like he could break if you looked at him too long. He reminds *me* of one of those miniature glass animals that your Grandma Edith used to set on her coffee table. Thin and clear and bony. The legs on those things snapped easier than matchsticks."

"He won't break, will he?" Dot asked, concerned.

"No baby of mine's going to break, sweetie," Mr. Vorlob guaranteed.

"We made a card for Mom," Adine said, pulling the card out from behind her back and handing it to her father. "Everyone helped."

"Aunt Irene wrote Effie's name for her," Dot told her father.

"Your mother will love this," Mr. Vorlob said, reading the card. "And it looks good enough to eat."

The card had been Adine's idea. They'd used uncooked macaroni and spaghetti, gluing the pasta onto a piece of folded construction paper in the shape of a stork. The spaghetti formed the stork's long, thin legs and his beak. The macaroni became the stork's massive body. Adine had written THIS IS A STORK under the mosaic, just to make sure that everyone knew what it was.

"I should really get back to the hospital, girls," Mr. Vorlob said. "I'm going to bring the Polaroid with me, so you'll all know what the baby looks like when I come home."

As he walked to the door, Mr. Vorlob was pelted with another barrage of questions: "What about the baby's name?" "When are they coming home?" "When are *you* coming home?"

"I'll be back soon . . . ," was all he said as he hurried out, the door swallowing his words when it slammed shut.

Adine thought she had a dream about a bear that night. The bear was friendly, and big as an overstuffed chair. He climbed into bed next to her, whispered something into her ear, and then settled down, his back facing hers like a bulky wall.

When Adine woke the next morning, her father was snoring beside her. Adine hadn't dreamed at all. The bear had been her father.

6

Breakfast

They finally came home.

Adine had been waiting at the living-room window, clinging to the drape as if she were part of it. She whooped when the bus pulled up in front of the house. "They're here!" she hollered. Mr. Vorlob got out of the bus first, moving backward, guiding his wife. He took her elbow and helped her up the walk to the porch. With both arms, Mrs. Vorlob held a small bundle close to her chest. The bundle was no larger than half a loaf of bread.

Aunt Irene and the girls ran out to the porch to greet them. "Careful with the door," cautioned Aunt Irene. "Close it quickly. Don't let Deedee out." The girls carried balloons and threw confetti. Inside, Deedee leaned on the front window, trying to attack the confetti as it twirled to the ground.

After hugs and kisses and peeks at the baby (and a look at the *F* wall), and more hugs and kisses and peeks, Mrs. Vorlob laid the baby down in the nursery and everyone went to the kitchen to eat. "We can look at the baby later," Mrs. Vorlob said. "Right now, I just want to sit and reacquaint myself with your old familiar faces. You know, if I had anything to say about it, I'd change the hospital visiting rules in a minute. I think children under twelve should be able to visit just like anyone else. One more day without seeing you guys and I don't know what I'd have done."

Adine didn't know what she would have done, either. All the phone calls with her mother and progress reports from her father and photos of her brother had little effect on the loneliness she had felt being separated. Adine had always missed her mother when she went to the hospital to have babies, but it had been worse this time. Worse because Aunt Irene had been there, rather than one of the neighborhood women, like usual. Worse because Mrs. Vorlob had gone in early, unexpectedly. Worse because she had stayed longer. Worse because Adine kept thinking that those things meant that something bad was happening, despite her parents' promises that everything was fine.

"I'm so glad you're home," Adine whispered to her mother.

"Me, too," Mrs. Vorlob whispered back.

• • •

The homecoming-celebration-breakfast was ready. Adine and Aunt Irene made M&M pancakes (plain and peanut), blueberry coffeecake, bacon, and scrambled eggs. There was milk, orange juice, and English muffins with strawberry jam, too. Aunt Irene mixed a few drops of blue food coloring in with the eggs because the baby was a boy, but the eggs ended up the color of pea soup. Marbled, chunky pea soup.

Everyone teased and commented about the eggs. Aunt Irene defended herself, saying, "They're unique and they're festive and they taste perfectly normal." But when the big serving bowl was passed around the table, most of the eggs remained where they were. "Well, it looks like Deedee is going to have a feast, too," Aunt Irene said, placing the bowl on the floor beside Deedee's personalized food and water dishes. Laughter filled the kitchen as Deedee, purring like a lawn mower, planted herself firmly in the bowl and began to eat.

• • •

Adine watched her mother closely throughout breakfast. Mrs. Vorlob's face was pale and
puffy, so that when she smiled it seemed her
mouth had to work harder to turn up at the
corners. But she smiled a lot. Everyone did.
Adine would remember that morning as a
morning filled with smiles. "If I could," said
Mrs. Vorlob, "I'd pickle this moment. Keep it
forever."

Adine had curled her hair early that morning;
she didn't care that no one had noticed. She
didn't mind when Effie slapped her English
muffin and a glob of jam landed on Adine's
shirt. Or when Dot accidentally knocked over
her milk and Adine ended up with a soaked lap.
Mrs. Vorlob was home. Having her back made
Adine feel warm and light. Almost bubbly. As
if part of her had been missing and now it was
replaced. And to have a new brother made the
circle of her life larger. Adine could have sat at
the round world of a table all day, the sunlight

spilling across them like a waterfall. Now, if only Aunt Irene would leave, she thought. Then everything would be perfect.

"I almost forgot," Mr. Vorlob said, rising. "We should have a toast." He poured more juice into everyone's glass. "To our new addition—" he said, after clearing his throat. "May he be as healthy, special, and lovable as each of his sisters."

Glasses clinked like bells.

Effie cooed and banged her squat plastic cup on the tray of her high chair. Orange juice splashed.

"When is the new addition going to be named?" Aunt Irene asked, reaching for the last strip of bacon on the platter.

"Yeah, when?" Carla said, excited.

"Yeah," everyone else echoed.

"Well," Mr. Vorlob said, making a tepee out of his napkin, "Mom and I talked about it and we're still not sure if the baby's name should begin with an *F* or not. It's just nice to have him home where he belongs. That's the main thing. So until we decide what to do, we thought we'd just call him Baby."

Mrs. Vorlob nodded.

"Baby?!" Adine said, giving a vomity look.

"Yuck," said Bernice. "That makes him sound like a doll or something."

"I can add him to my collection," Carla joked. "I bet he wets just like my doll Wanda. Maybe better."

"And he doesn't even need batteries," Bernice said, giggling.

Mrs. Vorlob reached into the pocket of her peppermint-striped jumper and pulled out a pack of cigarettes and her lighter. Adine frowned. She had hoped that her mother wouldn't take up smoking again. Pretend-smoking vegetables may have looked silly, but at least they didn't stink and they were good for you. TV commecials about cancer frightened Adine. Mrs. Vorlob lit a cigarette and took a long drag. Smoke streamed upward as she spoke. "Some of the other babies at the hospital *did* need batteries, so to speak. They were so tiny they couldn't live on their own. Baby's lucky—or I should say *we're* lucky that Baby's as healthy as he is. A few of the other preemies had enough wires and tubey things attached to them that they looked like miniature astronauts."

Adine imagined a whole crew of Cabbage Patch Preemies floating through outer space in suits of metallic silver, her tiny brother leading the way.

"Is Baby *retarded*?" Bernice asked, curling her upper lip.

"No, sweetie," Mrs. Vorlob said. "He's just little because he was born early. And he's special and bright and beautiful—like all of you."

The refrigerator was humming-buzzing in the corner, as if it were gossiping with the stove.

Mrs. Vorlob leaned back, tilting her chair. "When I was in the hospital," she said, "Dr.

Hunter told me I couldn't have any more children. Baby's our last."

"Why?" asked Carla.

"Well, I guess you could say my body just won't take it anymore."

"Like how your body won't take riding the roller coaster at Great America?" Bernice asked.

A grin cracked across Mrs. Vorlob's face. She eased her chair forward again, the front legs clipping the floor twice, like hooves. "Kind of, honey. But I can take pills so I can ride the roller coaster. I can't take pills to let me have more babies."

"But I thought we were going to have a baby for every letter in the alphabet!" said Dot. "*A, B, C, D, E, F, G . . . ,*" she sang.

Mr. Vorlob hooted until he coughed.

"Since Baby's our last," Mrs. Vorlob said, "we have to come up with something really special for his name. It's got to be perfect. I want to do something different with the nursery, too."

"You mean, we have to redo the *F* wall?" asked Adine.

"Well, maybe," answered Mrs. Vorlob. "You girls did such a nice job, though. Let's just wait and see."

"It's because Aunt Irene ruined it by putting that cat on it," Carla whispered loud enough for everyone to hear.

Aunt Irene shot Carla a toxic look.

Mrs. Vorlob crushed out her cigarette and got up. "Let's all go to the nursery and see how that new brother of yours is doing."

"Can I hold him?" Adine asked.

"Sure."

"Me, too?" asked Dot.

"Me! Me!" yelled Effie.

"You're not strong enough, silly," Carla said to Effie.

"*Every*one can hold him," said Mrs. Vorlob, as she pulled the old list of names off the refrigerator door and tossed it into the garbage pail by the sink. "Baby's as light as dandelion fuzz."

7

Baby

One by one, Adine, Bernice, Carla, Dot, Aunt Irene, and Mr. Vorlob, who was carrying Effie, filed into the nursery behind Mrs. Vorlob and crowded around the crib.

"Remember, he's very fragile," Mrs. Vorlob cautioned, hovering over the crib. "Be gentle."

Baby was curled up under a fluffy white

blanket, a sparrow hidden in a cloud. He was sleeping, his tiny breaths moving the blanket up and down ever so slightly. Mrs. Vorlob pulled the blanket back, giving everyone a full view. Something about him—his size, shape, posture—suddenly reminded Adine of the chickens that hung in the old butcher shop downtown.

"He's *ugly!*" Carla piped up, poking at Baby through the rails, over the bumper pad. "He's so—pink! And purpley! And he looks worse than in the pictures you took, Daddy."

"His head looks like a tomato," Bernice whispered.

"He's really, really, really little," Dot sang, tugging on her mother's striped jumper. "He could fit in the back of T. J. Deroucher's toy dump truck. The yellow one. The one he never shares."

Mrs. Vorlob nodded. "He's beautiful," she said, rubbing her finger around the edge of Baby's ear. "Beautiful."

"Can I do that?" Carla asked. She accidentally fell against the crib, her finger striking the side of Baby's head. Hard.

Baby wiggled. And moaned. The moans were barely audible. As if he wanted to cry, but couldn't quite manage it.

"Careful, Carla," Aunt Irene barked.

"Sorry, Mama," Carla said sheepishly, her bottom lip sticking out. "I didn't hurt him. Anyway, if people looked like worms, that's exactly what they'd look like."

"Don't be a smarty," Mr. Vorlob said, motioning for Carla to come to him. She stomped over to her father, her sunny red sandals clapping like applause. Mr. Vorlob set Effie down, picked Baby up, and knelt, holding Baby low enough so even Dot and Effie could see. Mr. Vorlob made gurgling noises and softly touched his nose to Baby's. Baby seemed to disappear in his father's thick, hairy arms. Mr. Vorlob's beard and deep voice were like weights pressing down on Baby's frail body. "Look, Carla," Mr.

Vorlob said, as quietly as he could. "Look what a little man your brother is. He's as perfect as can be. Perfect eyes, nose, mouth. Perfect ears, fingers, toes," he continued, lightly kissing everything he mentioned. They all took turns holding Baby and kissing each of his toes. Then Mr. Vorlob placed Baby back in the crib.

"Okay, troops," Mr. Vorlob said, scratching his beard. "I've got a project that needs attention." His dark eyes flashed. "Follow me."

Mr. Vorlob led Bernice, Carla, Dot, and Effie out of the nursery toward the kitchen.

"Can I stay with you, Mom?" Adine asked.

"Scoot," Aunt Irene said firmly, pointing Adine in the direction of the door, with a dismissive push. "Give your mother and me some time alone. We need it."

I need time alone with her, Adine thought. She's *my* mother. Tears burned hot in Adine's eyes as she closed the nursery door, wishing she remained behind it.

• • •

Mr. Vorlob's project was to cart the flowers and cards that Mrs. Vorlob had received at the hospital from the bus into the living room. There was a shopful, and the back of the bus smelled like a parlor crammed with old ladies, each wearing a distinct perfume: rose, lilac, lily of the valley.

Adine thought some of the arrangements were beautiful—the globe of peach tea roses in the pewter bowl and the yellow daisies cascading from the white wicker basket. Others, she thought were questionable, particularly the planter from Mrs. Vorlob's bowling team. The planter was in the shape of a bowling ball, large and black. It was filled with orange plastic tulips and green plastic leaves that looked like knives. The plastic smelled like K Mart. Gross.

They placed the flowers on the floor, on the end tables, on the hutch. The cards—decorated

with teddy bears, rattles, and blue baby boot-
ies—were lined up in between.

When the bus was empty, the living room
reminded Adine of church when someone dies.

"Lookit this one," Bernice said, holding up a
ceramic pot decorated with primitive-looking
cats. "I'll bet it's from Aunt Irene."

Who else? Adine thought. The pot held an
azalea plant, heavy with lavender blossoms.
And when no one was watching, Adine
grabbed one of the blossoms and snapped it off.

That night, Adine did spend time alone with
her mother. With her mother and Baby. Dinner was over. Everyone else was playing Chutes
and Ladders in the kitchen. Adine didn't mind
missing out at all. She wasn't terribly fond of
playing games with a lot of people. Especially
with her sisters and her aunt. Bernice and Carla
usually ended up cheating. Dot usually lost in-
terest and quit. And Aunt Irene was too bossy.

Sometimes she'd even slap your hand if you accidently grabbed the dice out of turn. But every now and then, Adine played games alone. For hours. She'd make up exotic names for the different playing pieces (Selena, Dominique, Juanita), keeping track of how many games each player won on a pad of paper. *That* was the way to play games.

"He's really cute, isn't he?" Mrs. Vorlob said.

"Yeah," Adine replied, smiling at her brother.

The three of them were on the floor in the nursery. Baby was lying on his stomach on the middle of a large blue blanket, a pinkish island surrounded by an ocean. Adine and Mrs. Vorlob were on either side.

Adine didn't know how long they had been there. She was daydreaming. Looking at the fairy on the *F* wall, the falling star. Looking at her mother, at Baby. Adine heard voices from the kitchen periodically: Bernice and Carla—

screaming, Dot—singing, Effie—cooing, Mr.
Vorlob—laughing, and Aunt Irene—bellow-
ing. Adine was happy to be where she was. She
placed her hands on her stomach and wondered
what it would be like to have a baby. One
night, while Mrs. Vorlob was in the hospital,
Adine had taken a pillow from the couch and
stuffed it under her shirt. It had felt funny.

"Do you smell what I smell?" asked Mrs.
Vorlob.

Adine did. "I think so," she said, giggling.

"Then it's time to go to work."

Mrs. Vorlob pulled Baby's dirty Pampers off
and quickly wiped him. Adine sprinkled pow-
der on him and secured the fresh, puffy diaper
around his thin waist.

Adine picked Baby up; the Pampers slid
down. Mrs. Vorlob tried her best to tighten it.
"This'll have to do," she said, gently bouncing
Baby. "Grow," she said to him with a grin.

Adine thought he grinned back.

Before Mrs. Vorlob laid Baby down for the night, Adine placed her head over Baby and sniffed under his chin. She loved the way Baby smelled (except when his diapers were dirty). Clean and white and light. The small amount of hair he had was dark and fine. Adine cupped her hand over it like a helmet. "Good night, Alexander," she whispered.

"*Alexander?*" said Mrs. Vorlob.

"Well," Adine explained, "I thought that if we gave Baby an *A* name, because he's the first boy, that I'd vote for Alexander. It sounds important. If I was a boy, I'd want a name like that."

"Sounds hoity-toity to me," said Mrs. Vorlob. "Al is a nice name, though. Simple and to the point."

Adine instantly became aware that her mother's taste in boys' names was similar to her taste in girls'. She wasn't surprised.

"Adine," Mrs. Vorlob said peaceably, reaching

for the rolled-up diaper to throw away, "tomorrow Aunt Irene will be bringing some more things over from her apartment. She told me today that your Uncle Gilly is getting married soon to someone in Iowa. She's a little upset. She asked if we'd mind if she ended up staying longer than we had planned."

Adine swallowed. She didn't know what to say.

"Will you do this for me, Adine? Think of it as a favor for *me*, not Irene."

Adine nodded and looked away. She blinked hard, holding back tears.

Mrs. Vorlob rested her arm on Adine's shoulders and sighed. "What a day this has been, huh?"

Adine said nothing.

"I guess I just made a major understatement," Mrs. Vorlob admitted, her voice less gravelly than usual.

There was a sudden burst of laughter from the kitchen.

"Well, Adine, what do you say we go play a game of Chutes and Ladders? We can be a team and beat their pants off."

Adine didn't want to, but she said she would, anyway.

And as they walked down the narrow hallway to the kitchen, Mrs. Vorlob winked at Adine. As if they shared some ancient secret.

8

The Flowers

Aunt Irene was taking over. Everything. Boxes of her belongings were stacked under the window in Adine's bedroom, and her outlandish clothes now took up half the space in Adine's shallow closet. Aunt Irene set up a TV tray beside Adine's bed; placed atop the tray were some of her choice porcelain cats and dozens of bottles of nail polish. Knickknacks littered the windowsill. Aunt Irene even smoked a whole pack of her horrible brown cigarettes in Adine's room one afternoon as she sorted through her boxes, causing the small, cramped space—and everything in it—to reek, in Adine's opinion.

When Adine quietly grumbled, Aunt Irene swung back the curtains and heaved the window open. "Your mother smokes," she said crisply.

"But never in my room," Adine explained, staring at the floor.

To make sure she wouldn't do it again, Adine lettered two NO SMOKING signs with felt-tip markers and taped them on either side of her door. Adine even contemplated drawing a dead cat with a burning cigarette lying beside it on the signs, but decided against it.

If Aunt Irene saw Adine kiss Baby (eyes, nose, and mouth), she'd say, "Don't slobber on your brother—you'll suffocate him."

If Adine wanted to use the telephone to call the weather recording for the local report (to see if a storm was forecast), most likely Aunt Irene was talking to one of her friends about Uncle Gilly. For hours.

Aunt Irene hogged the TV, and once, when there were only ten minutes left of a "Gilligan's Island" rerun, Aunt Irene made Adine, Bernice, and Carla go to the kitchen to do the lunch dishes.

"I'm telling Mama," Carla threatened.

"Don't bother your mother, girls," Aunt Irene said with authority, plopping down in front of the TV and switching stations to "Days of Our Lives." "She's busy with your brother."

It was always the same story when Adine complained. "She needs us right now," Mrs. Vorlob kept saying. "Bear with her," Mr. Vorlob would add. Why can't she have children of her own to torment? Adine continued to wonder.

Dot and Effie liked having Aunt Irene around. All Aunt Irene had to do to keep them happy was to perform her train impersonation a few times daily. And Baby, of course, didn't seem to mind one way or the other. About anything. Young children, Adine decided, are easy to deceive.

Bernice and Carla went into business. Furtively. They sold their mother's flowers from the hospital to their friends. Roses for a quarter. Carnations for fifteen cents. Daisies and all others for a dime. They also sold peeks at Baby, when they knew their mother was busy elsewhere. A penny for a quick look, a nickel for a longer one, and a dime if he happened to be drooling. Business was booming; by the end of the week they had earned three dollars and sixty-three cents.

It was Aunt Irene who put an end to their enterprise. One afternoon, as she and Adine were folding laundry, they overheard Carla sneak T. J. Deroucher into the nursery and demand a nickel in a fierce whisper. Then Carla sold him two roses and immediately made him give them back to her since she was his girl friend.

"Thank you, T. J.," Carla said sweetly, putting the flowers back in their vase to sell again. She pecked his cheek.

T. J. blushed and looked confused. He jammed his fists deep into his pockets.

"Why don't you buy some roses for your mom?" Carla asked.

"Out of money," T. J. answered, swaying back and forth, shifting from one foot to the other.

"And *you're* out of business, Carla Celeste Vorlob!" Aunt Irene roared, storming around the corner from where she and Adine had been watching. Aunt Irene made Carla return T. J.'s money.

"You're not going to tell Mama and Daddy, are you, Auntie?" Carla asked with supplicating eyes.

"Don't tempt me. You're just lucky your mother's napping and your father's at work."

"I gave her seventy-five cents yesterday," T. J. told Aunt Irene. "And a dime the day before."

Adine giggled as she stacked towels. Carla and Bernice's commercial venture was just one of many schemes they never ceased to think of. Adine doubted if she could ever come up with the ideas they did, much less carry them out. When Mrs. Vorlob talked about Carla and Bernice, she often said they were creative and spontaneous. Adine thought that *she* was creative, in a different way, though; she loved to draw and was good at it. But she knew she wasn't spontaneous.

That afternoon, Carla and Bernice paraded from door to door in the neighborhood, emptying their milk carton of change. Aunt Irene ordered Adine to go with them to make sure they returned all the money at the proper houses. Adine thought her role as supervisor was unfair; she hadn't done anything wrong. Adine (tugging her ear) waited at the front sidewalk while her sisters reluctantly marched up to each porch. Adine kicked the weeds and scanned the sky. The large cloud following them was in the shape of Aunt Irene (if you stretched your imagination); the mass next to it was a giant, pointy sword. Adine stared at them until they merged—the sword jutting right into Aunt Irene's stomach.

On the way back home, the three of them decided that something had to be done before Aunt Irene took complete control.

"She's so *bossy*," said Adine.

"Like she's our mother or something," said Bernice. "We have to think of something good."

"I've got an idea," Carla said in a hushed, secretive voice, her eyes narrowing to slits. Then she ran ahead and started skipping. "A great one!" she yelled.

They began working on Carla's idea immediately. They bolted to Bernice and Carla's room and closed the door. Carla's idea was to draw pictures of Aunt Irene and Deedee, using Adine's felt-tip markers. The more unflattering the better. Then they'd place the pictures in strategic locations around the house (where Aunt Irene would hopefully find them, and where Mr. and Mrs. Vorlob hopefully wouldn't). "Don't you get it," Bernice had explained, crouching between her sisters. "After she sees them, she'll *want* to leave." Bernice thought that a few signs were in order, too.

Although Adine had liked the idea just minutes earlier, her enthusiasm was quickly waning once she actually started to draw.

"How's this?" Bernice asked, leaning back so Adine could read the sign she had just finished. It said WE ONLY HAVE ONE MOTHER AND HER NAME IS *NOT* IRENE.

Adine nodded.

Carla was working on two drawings of Deedee at the same time. A "before" picture and an "after" picture. The "before" picture showed Deedee eating out of her dish, an enormous steam roller headed directly for her. The "after" picture simply showed a flat, gray-and-black blob, surrounded by a pool of red.

"Oooh, that's *good!*" said Bernice, excited.

"Can you tell the red gunk is cat blood?" Carla asked.

"Of course," said Bernice. "But you could make a *little* more blood, though."

"What are you working on, Adine?" Carla asked, craning her neck to see.

"It's not that good," Adine remarked, holding up her drawing. It was a portrait of Aunt Irene as a train—big and square and sturdy. Adine had drawn her stooped on a railroad track, toothless, with a smokestack sprouting out of her head. Black smoke spewed out of the smokestack, and out of her nose and ears, as well. Adine colored the train like Aunt Irene's loudest dress.

Bernice and Carla shrieked with delight.

"That's the best!" Bernice said. "It's exactly what she looks like. Honestly."

"That dress part is funny," Carla observed. "Just like the real one Aunt Irene wears. I really like how you have the smoke coming out of her ears, too. Ha!"

"Why don't we put that one under her pillow?" Bernice suggested. "Maybe we should put them *all* under her pillow," she added, using her hands for emphasis. "That way, Mom and Dad won't see them."

"Unless Auntie's a tattletale, too," Carla said.

"I don't know," Adine said slowly. During moments like these, Adine didn't feel like the oldest.

"Aw, come on," Bernice coaxed. "Let's do it!"

Carla grinned evilly and nodded, her eyebrows wiggling on her forehead mischievously.

"All right," Adine whispered hesitantly.

And so, without much deliberation it was

decided: Adine would slide the thin stack of drawings and messages under Aunt Irene's pillow that night.

Adine was waiting. And waiting. And waiting. She had slipped the drawings under Aunt Irene's pillow and zipped back to the cot. That was half an hour ago, and still Aunt Irene hadn't come to bed. Adine's heart was moving with the speed and force of a jackhammer. She tried to compose herself and fall asleep. She couldn't. She kept thinking of her drawing of Aunt Irene. The more she thought about it, the more it seemed like something Gary Wilker would do. And that thought made her hate what she had done, despite the fact that she hated having Aunt Irene around. Regret swept over Adine like a tidal wave and whooshed through her as if a kite were tied to her heart.

But still she waited. And waited. And waited. Every creak in the hallway, every shadow that skimmed across the floor caused

Adine to flinch. She pulled the covers over her head and told herself how terrible and selfish her aunt was. How bossy and embarrassing. How eccentric.

Adine turned over on her stomach. She rolled to her side. Lay on her back. She heard Aunt Irene's voice. Coming closer. Closer. Adine gulped, took a deep breath, and jumped up. She grabbed the drawings, rolled them up, and flung them under her dresser just as Aunt Irene opened the door.

"You should be sleeping, little lady," Aunt Irene snapped.

Adine flopped down on the cot with a thud and a sigh. "I am," she whispered.

9

The Blouse

When Aunt Irene's presence wasn't command-
ing all of Adine's attention, thinking of a name
for Baby and deciding how to decorate the
nursery consumed her thoughts. Everyone
else's, too. If they weren't going to keep the *F*
wall, Adine thought that all the walls in the
nursery would look best painted one solid,
peaceful color. Light peach or yellowish. Soft

and creamy like butter, as if the walls would melt if you happened to bump into them. But Adine was especially determined to come up with a suitable name for her brother. Mrs. Vorlob still hadn't decided what letter Baby's name should begin with, so Adine just tried to think of nice-sounding names, regardless of how they were spelled. She searched everywhere—in books, the telephone directory, the newspaper, even in the pantry (where she discovered two distinct possibilities: Campbell—from the cans of soup, and Duncan—from a cake mix), and under the bathroom sink (where she momentarily considered Lysol as a name, before dismissing the idea as being ridiculous).

Holding Baby, Adine whispered name after name in his ear, hoping he'd somehow respond favorably to one of them—with a turn of the head, a flutter of his thin lilac eyelids, a pucker of agreement on his lips. But time after time he gave no sign to indicate a preference.

When she was alone with Baby, Adine

pretended that she was his mother. She imagined herself in a smart red dress (like the picture in the Sears catalogue she had torn out and kept folded in her underwear drawer), strolling with Baby in the outlet mall near the interstate. People would stop her to steal a look at her child, saying: "What a gorgeous baby!" and "I've never seen a more beautiful child." Adine would blush. "Thank you," she'd say, covering her baby and hurrying on.

Denise Gackstetter and her mother came to visit. The Gackstetters lived down the block and around the corner. Denise and Adine were in the same class. Whenever anyone asked Adine, she would say that Denise was her best friend. Last year, in school, they sat side by side in the back of the room because their teacher, Mr. Pavilonis, said that they were well behaved and didn't act up like Gary Wilker and Mary Rose Wampole, who sat in the front. They both were bashful—sometimes with each other—and their time spent together was often quiet. Reading books on the porch, doing homework at each other's houses during the school year, riding bikes, drawing.

Aunt Irene said that Denise and her parents were "artsy-fartsy." Denise was good in art, but Adine knew that that wasn't what Aunt Irene was referring to. Adine couldn't quite pinpoint what "artsy-fartsy" meant, but Adine guessed it had something to do with the fact that Denise's mother had a colored streak in her hair, which she periodically changed from orange to pink to blue, and that Denise's father wore a small gold earring in one of his ears. Denise had pierced ears, too. Three holes in one ear, two in the other, always filled by tiny silver hoops.

Adine was a bit envious of Denise; although she'd never wear a total of five earrings, herself, Adine desperately wished that she could have pierced ears. She had wished that for at least four years. Her parents said that she had to wait until she was twelve. Adine never pressed the point.

When Denise and her mother entered the Vorlobs' house, Aunt Irene focused on Mrs. Gackstetter's hair, which was currently tinted maroon, for a few seconds and rolled her eyes and clucked her tongue before saying hello. Considering how Aunt Irene dressed and acted, Adine didn't think that her aunt had any right to pass judgment.

After looking at Baby, Mrs. Gackstetter and Mrs. Vorlob went to the kitchen to smoke cigarettes and drink coffee, and Denise went with Adine to Adine's room to draw. Denise usually drew pictures of animals (horses being her favorite). Adine usually drew pictures of families and made up names for each person. She neatly lettered their names along the bottom of each drawing.

"That's a nice horse," Adine told Denise.

"Thanks. It's supposed to be an Appaloosa," Denise said. She pointed to the fancy dress

Adine had drawn on one of her people. "I like that outfit."

Next, Adine drew a picture of some of her mother's flowers. Denise drew a picture of a baby. She held it up to show Adine. "I asked my mom if we could have a baby. She said having one baby was enough for her. You're lucky, Adine. My mom says she doesn't know how your mom does it."

"But sometimes it must be nice to have it be just you and your mom and your dad."

Denise shrugged. "Sometimes they watch me too much and check on me every five minutes. Like *I'm* a baby."

Adine thought that getting that much attention might be nice. Adine also thought that being an only child would minimize the wear and tear on her felt-tip markers. Bernice and Carla often used Adine's markers without asking, and they had a tendency to press too hard, squashing the tips and fraying them. Sometimes, they even left the caps off, drying them out. Denise's markers, it seemed to Adine, were always pointy and sharp, the colors vibrant.

They drew separately and silently until they collaborated on a drawing of Gary Wilker. Adine drew his head twice as large as it should have been and colored it red. Denise drew his body twice as small and colored it green. They gave him elephant ears, duck feet, and pimples everywhere they could fit them.

The drawing of Gary Wilker reminded Adine of her drawing of Aunt Irene. Adine had hidden all of the drawings and signs in her closet under a box of old toys. When Bernice and Carla had asked how Aunt Irene had reacted, Adine had simply said, "She didn't say anything." Adine couldn't tell her sisters that she had chickened out, that Aunt Irene had never even seen the drawings.

For days after, Bernice and Carla kept trying to lure Aunt Irene into talking about the drawings.

"Do you think we're good drawers, Auntie?" Carla asked in a sugary voice.

"Do older people ever find anything under their pillows, Aunt Irene?" Bernice asked with a theatrical air. "You know, like things from the tooth fairy or someone?"

Aunt Irene obviously never gave them the answers they wanted. And obviously, Carla's scheme didn't drive Aunt Irene away.

Adine felt guilty about the picture of Aunt Irene all over again, but not about the one of Gary Wilker.

Denise and Adine giggled until they laughed. And they laughed until they got hiccups. Adine got up and shut her bedroom door, to keep things quiet for Baby. They broke into laughter again, loud and long.

"Whose is *that*?" Denise asked, gesturing to one of Aunt Irene's chiffon cat blouses hanging by a hook on the back of Adine's door.

"My aunt's," Adine mumbled.

"It's gross."

"It's not *that* bad," Adine lied. She hated it. The blouse was yellow. A big black cat with an arched back and olive eyes wrapped itself around the blouse, from the front left-hand pocket, across the back, to the front right-hand pocket.

"My dad calls your aunt a character," Denise said. "He says every family's got at least one. She makes him laugh." Denise took the blouse off the hook and held it up in front of herself. "Yuck."

Adine tugged on her ear. She realized that what Denise had just said was true, but it left Adine confused. At that moment, Adine's feelings for her aunt were a jumbled mess, just like the "junk drawer" in the pantry, which held a thick tangle of rusty nails, yarn snippets, wire, string, small pieces of multicolored thread, scraps of material, crumbs and—if you searched thoroughly enough—pennies, nickels, and shiny buttons.

Adine tried to ignore Denise's comments. "Come on," Adine said. "Why don't we draw a picture of Mary Rose Wampole? We can make her worse than Gary Wilker."

For a split second while they drew, Adine pretended that the picture was of Denise, rather than Mary Rose Wampole.

A few days later, while she was hunting in her closet for an old toy to give to Baby, Adine discovered that the stack of signs and drawings of Aunt Irene and Deedee was missing. Her heart beat in her throat and her stomach instantly went heavy, like the time she ate seven cookies right before bed.

"Oh, no," Adine whispered to herself. "What am I going to do now?"

10

Names

Baby grew. Not much. And not quickly. But Adine could tell that he was getting bigger. At least she thought so. She tried to keep track of his height with her father's yardstick, but could rarely make Baby lie straight enough to get an accurate measurement. Mrs. Vorlob had explained to Adine what a soft spot on a baby's head was, and where it was located on Baby.

Sometimes Adine could swear it had grown harder; other times it seemed softer.

Even though Baby was the Vorlobs' first boy, there wasn't much they had to buy for him. There were enough blocks and dolls and cars and dress-up clothes and baseball gloves hiding in the closets and chests to keep him occupied when he was ready for them. The Vorlobs owned one hundred eighty-two Fisher-Price people and twenty-six stuffed animals.

Baby usually wore Pampers and plain, hand-me-down T-shirts, unless his sisters had him all decked out in their doll clothes or he was wearing his sleeveless Sylvester undershirt from Aunt Irene.

Mr. Vorlob took photos of Baby, and Adine wrote captions under them: in the back of T. J. Deroucher's dump truck (HEAVY LOAD!), camouflaged in a pile of Carla's dolls with sunglasses and a too-big Brewers cap on (ONE IN A MILLION), and stark naked, getting a bath in Mrs. Vorlob's spaghetti pot (WHAT'S

COOKING?). But most of the photos were of Baby sleeping in his crib, because that's what he mostly did.

"When are we going to name him?" everyone kept asking.

Mrs. Vorlob just kept shrugging.

Before the tornado siren completed its first sounding, everyone was down in the basement, in the dark, cobwebbed hollow beneath the stairs. Mr. Vorlob brought the transistor radio with him. Mrs. Vorlob brought Baby and a couple of boxes of Jell-O for the girls to share while they waited for the warning to be lifted. Adine, Bernice, Carla, Dot, and Effie stuck their fingers into the colored sugar, then licked their fingers and kissed them clean. Over and over. Aunt Irene did, too. They could only eat Jell-O in that manner on special occasions. And they always had to brush their teeth twice, directly afterward.

Storms always seemed to excite everyone.

Everyone but Adine, of course. While her sisters sang and chanted ("It's raining, it's pouring, the old man is snoring . . . "), Adine's face grew tight as a fist and then she momentarily went dizzy. Adine had known a storm was coming. She knew by the way things smelled outside—musty and dull and fishy like new bedsheets from the outlet mall. She knew because the sky had been the color of tin all afternoon. She knew because after Willard Scott did the national weather on the "Today" show and then broke to the local station, the newscaster predicted the threat of a tornado in the area. And she knew because the insides of her stomach were bouncing around the way they always did when something like this was going to happen.

Once, a few summers earlier, Mr. Vorlob asked Adine to go with him when he left the basement to check the sky out the back-door window. "It's okay," he assured her. "The radio says the storm's passed." Adine clutched his arm with both hands, like a wrench. The sky was the color of dirty bathwater, the densely packed clouds still rolling swift and slick as dolphins, the backyard trees still struggling against the wind. Leaves were scattered like confetti. Before everything became still and sunny again, a single leaf caught Adine's eye as it leaped across the yard. She imagined herself as the leaf—tiny, tossing and turning, powerless against the wind.

When the threatening weather would pass, the girls would run out of the basement and compare their stories of how they spent their time in exile with their neighbors' versions. It always took Adine longer to adjust. Sometimes it seemed as if she moved in slow motion.

"Before the storm's over, why don't we try to come up with a name for Baby?" Aunt Irene suggested, swatting at a cobweb. "It'll help pass the time," she sniffed.

"We can try," Mrs. Vorlob replied, bouncing Baby on her hip.

"It can't hurt," Mr. Vorlob said. He lowered the volume on the radio. Adine moved closer to it, so as not to miss anything. She really wanted to concentrate on names—take her mind off the storm—but she wouldn't risk not being able to hear the radio if something important was announced.

They took turns calling out names while the wind and rain battered the house.

"T. J.!" Carla shouted.

"No," said Mrs. Vorlob.

"Campbell?" said Adine.

Mrs. Vorlob shook her head no.

"How about Felix or Sylvester?" Aunt Irene offered.

Baby spit up.

"I like the sound of Roland, Jr.," Mr. Vorlob said, smiling.

No.

"Duncan?" said Adine.

No.

"Mickey?"

No.

"Donald?"

No.

"Winnie, as in Pooh?" "Oscar?" "Grover?" "Bert?" "Ernie?" "Wilbur?"

No. No. No. No. No. No.

"George Washington Vorlob!"

No!

"Why don't we keep his name Baby?" Mr. Vorlob asked everyone, raising and lowering his eyebrows.

"*No!*" they all shouted, drowning out the sounds of the storm.

By the time the wind had died down and the sky was clear, they were no closer to finding a name for Baby. Nothing sounded exactly right to Mrs. Vorlob. And, except for her own suggestions, everything sounded completely wrong to Adine.

June had become July. July had turned into August. August was nearly September.

In the mornings, the dew was thick now—
the lawn a silver, beaded carpet. At night,
Adine often needed more than a sheet to keep
her warm. The county fair came and went, as
did the circus. School started. Uncle Gilly got
married in Iowa and sent a picture of his new
bride; she looked much thinner than Aunt Irene
and three times younger. Her name was
Charlene. Aunt Irene remained with the
Vorlobs, moving in more and more of her pos-
sessions. Consequently, Adine tugged on her
ear so frequently now, that she worried about
pulling it off. And Baby was still called Baby.

11

The Pixie

The Indian-summer moon was huge and yellow. Adine admired it through the filmy, half-opened window of the bus. It was one of the most beautiful things she had ever seen. Mr. Vorlob had taken Adine and her sisters to the Dairy Queen and for a ride on the wealthy side of town to gape at the big houses. Aunt

Irene and Deedee had come with them. Mrs. Vorlob had stayed home with Baby.

Periodically, Mr. Vorlob would beep the horn and wave wildly at strangers walking by, to see how they'd respond. Carla joined him—waving, and screaming, "Hello, happy Friday night!"—until she dropped her ice-cream cone out the window. Adine shrank down into the seat—greeting strangers like this embarrassed her. She couldn't bear to watch the passersby tilt their heads in confusion as a clunky, lime-green school bus offered noisy salutations.

Adine stared at the moon again as they snaked their way around a curve into Adine's favorite neighborhood. Adine had just learned in science class that the moon shone by reflecting the sun's light, that it revolved around the earth, and that it was spherical. But that night it appeared to be flat, like a tiddlywink suspended in midair.

Adine's favorite house in Mason was a mansion

near the lake. At night, it looked like a wedding cake under spotlights—three stories tall, all white, with carvings above the windows like frosting and a columned, wraparound porch with pink steps that spread out in three directions. The house seemed to be laughing, the shadows of the nearby trees bouncing across it and playing on the uneven turrets that crowned it.

To draw it all in, Adine usually begged her father to park by the overgrown field near the mansion. There was always too much to see whizzing by. But that night they just drove on, Adine keeping silent.

If Mrs. Vorlob had been along, they'd have played a game they called Who Lives Here? Adine loved the game. For every house fancy enough to warrant attention, Mrs. Vorlob would call out, "Who lives here?" The children would take turns making up a history for the people who lived in the houses. Names, jobs, number of children, pets. The bigger the house, the more unbelievable and imaginative the stories. Even if they'd pick the same houses time after time, the stories would always change.

It was much too hot for October in Mason, Wisconsin. Adine fidgeted in her seat, her bare legs sticking to the black vinyl. As much as she enjoyed viewing the houses and picturing herself living in them, Adine was ready to go home. The night was almost muggy, and Aunt Irene had been smoking the entire time, causing Adine's head to pound. When they passed street lamps, the smoke could be seen hanging in the feeble light of the bus like fog.

Deedee (thank goodness) was asleep on Aunt Irene's lap. Effie was asleep, too, her chocolate-mustached face leaning on Adine's slumped shoulder.

It was odd to see Aunt Irene directly behind Adine's father, in the seat where Mrs. Vorlob always sat. Mr. Vorlob still had his work clothes on. He was a pattern maker, and when he came home at four o'clock every day, you could tell he had worked hard—he looked as if he had been hosed down from top to bottom with sweat and dirt. Adine wasn't exactly sure what a pattern maker did, but she knew it didn't have anything to do with dress patterns. She used to think that when she was Dot's age.

They passed the Pixie Cleaners on East Street. A neon pixie fluttered above the building, flashing like a pulse. The pixie reminded Adine of the fairy on the *F* wall. Adine wished the fairy would come to life, wave her wand, and make Aunt Irene go back home to her own apartment (along with everything she had stuffed into Adine's room). Better yet, make her disappear. Forever. Baby had been home for months, and except for not having a real name, he was perfectly fine—small, but fine. In Adine's opinion, Aunt Irene wasn't needed. She wasn't needed at all. And it didn't seem to Adine that Aunt Irene needed the Vorlobs (although that's what Adine's mother kept saying).

If you really needed someone, you wouldn't be cranky and bossy and demanding. You'd be grateful to the people who were supposedly helping you. Adine didn't understand Aunt Irene, and she had a hard time liking things she didn't understand. In that respect, Adine put math and Aunt Irene in the same category.

As they sped down the street, Adine turned her head to catch a last glimpse of the pixie. When it was out of her vision, Adine closed her eyes and the pixie blinked in her mind.

The faint odor of paint met them as they walked into the house. Baby, in his crib, had been wheeled into the living room. The windows were all open and the portable fan was turning its head, whirring, ventilating the air for Baby.

Adine followed Mr. Vorlob upstairs and down the hall, the paint smell growing stronger. They entered the nursery. Mrs. Vorlob was facing the *F* wall, splashing white paint across it with a large brush. Everything was disappearing—the fairy, the falling star, the frogs, the farm. Without turning, Mrs. Vorlob continued—dipping her brush in the paint can, raising it with a slight flourish, and hiding the mural beneath a slick coat of white.

12

Stripes

"He's going to be a Z!" Mrs. Vorlob said excitedly, laying her brush down on the lid of the paint can. "Baby's name is going to begin with the letter Z!"

Before anyone could ask a question, Mrs. Vorlob continued, her paint-flecked hands a frenzy of gestures. "It just hit me like a ton of cinder blocks. While you were all out looking at the fancy houses, Baby woke up. I lulled him back to sleep by reading to him—that old alphabet book we've had for years. Of course, I always substitute you girls' names for *A, B, C, D,* and *E.* Well, I was going through, page after page, naming all the pictures like always, and when I got to *Z,* I thought, Wouldn't it be perfect if Baby's name began with a *Z?* Then there'd be Vorlobs from *A* to *Z.* Don't you see? Everything would be complete. Absolutely perfect."

Mrs. Vorlob lit a cigarette and blew smoke out in rings that wavered and grew wider as they rose. "I'm surprised I didn't think of it sooner," she said. "I must read that alphabet book to Baby a million times a day."

Everyone liked the idea.

Adine started thinking immediately. Zachary, she said to herself. Zachary. It sounded wonderful.

"So now we have to do a *Z* wall, right?" asked Bernice.

"Well, not exactly," said Mrs. Vorlob. "Even though I loved the *F* wall and all the other murals we've done, I thought it might be fun to try something different this time, seeing as it's our last. That's why I'm painting the *F* wall white." Mrs. Vorlob paused and reached for the alphabet book from on top of Baby's dresser. She turned to the last page in the book and held it up. There was a bold black letter *Z* in the upper left-hand corner, and a magnificent zebra filling up the rest of the page, its stripes running off the edges of the paper as if the book couldn't quite contain it.

Adine recognized the picture instantly; she'd seen it time and time again.

"See," Mrs. Vorlob explained, pointing to the illustration, then blocking off the zebra's head with her arm. "I thought we could paint gigantic zebra stripes—from ceiling to floor—across the entire wall that used to be the *F* wall. Just one big design."

Mrs. Vorlob twinkled about the nursery,

wielding her cigarette as if it were a magic wand, indicating where she wanted the stripes to be painted. The fairy from the *F* wall was gone forever, but there was a new one present. And she was as robust and real as the old one had been dainty and inanimate.

"I love this idea!" Mrs. Vorlob said with exuberance. She smiled so broadly that the skin around her eyes wrinkled.

Mrs. Vorlob wanted to repaint all the furniture in the nursery, too—metallic silver. "And if we can find one for a reasonable price," she added, "I'd like to buy a chrome crib."

The proposed decor of the room struck Adine as being a bit different, but that wasn't her main concern at the moment. "I'll get some paper," Adine offered eagerly, halfway out the door. "To make a list of *Z* names to hang on the refrigerator." Adine planned on writing ZACHARY right on top of the list, using neat, capital letters. She could picture it already—ZACHARY —in black on white.

"Wait, honey," Mrs. Vorlob called, motioning for Adine to come back. "That's the other thing I'd like to do differently. Because Baby's my last child and because Aunt Irene's my only sister—and doesn't have any children of her own—I'd like *her* to name Baby. I'd like Aunt Irene to give Baby a nice Z name." A pause. "If that's okay with everyone."

Mr. Vorlob nodded solemnly. And smiled.

Aunt Irene's face turned flush with happiness. She galumphed over to Mrs. Vorlob, banging into furniture, and hugged her. Mrs. Vorlob returned the embrace, their arms entwined like pretzels.

Adine felt something like jealousy well up inside her, and she nearly choked on it. But what could she say?

Bernice groaned.

Carla said exactly what Adine was thinking: "What if we hate it? What if it's a lousy name? What if she wants to call him *Zorro*?"

"Don't worry," said Aunt Irene. "I've got good taste."

Compared to what? thought Adine. In her mind, the sheet of paper with ZACHARY written on it was torn into tiny pieces and blown away. Bits scattering in the wind. Gone forever.

"To bed with all of you," Mr. Vorlob ordered, glancing at his watch. "It's late. Get a good rest so we can all get up bright and early and paint."

After more hugging with Aunt Irene, Mrs. Vorlob lit another cigarette. "Tomorrow we're going to stripe this room!" she said. She did a little twist and softly bumped her behind to Adine's.

Adine barely noticed. She was listening to Dot, who was toddling to the bathroom. "Zorro, Zorro, Zorro," she sang. "My brother's name is Zorro. . . ."

The next morning they painted. Enormous, jagged zebra stripes (from ceiling to floor) on the wall in the nursery. It wasn't nearly as much fun as doing the *F* wall had been. Instead of having many colors to choose from, this time there was only black. A black as glossy and dense as oil.

Adine worked diligently; this was serious business. Bernice and Carla gave each other thick black mustaches. Then they dribbled paint on Deedee as she scurried to the window in pursuit of a squirrel dillydallying on a utility wire outside. Dot was pretending, using her paintbrush as a microphone. "Pretty black stripes," she chirped, taking tiny sidesteps, facing everyone. "Pretty, pretty stripes. . . ."

When they were done, and Adine stood back to get a good look at the finished product, it occurred to her that the wall was a bit like a giant, flattened candy cane. It also occurred to Adine that if you looked at the wall too long, the stripes began to vibrate. She knew she'd hate waking up to the zebra stripes every morning. She'd be dizzy before she even got out of bed. Poor Baby. This room belongs in a punk rocker's house, Adine thought. She had seen photos in magazines near the checkout lines at the grocery store of people dressed in leather, with spiked hair and safety pins through their ears. This nursery should belong to people like that, she concluded.

Mr. Vorlob ran his fingers through his beard, leaning his head to and fro, and squinting. "Looks great," he said after a few minutes.

"Ooo-la-la," said Mrs. Vorlob, spreading her arms out like an umbrella opening. "It's the *zebra* wall. Now all we need is a name for Baby." She turned toward Aunt Irene.

"Still thinking," Aunt Irene said vaguely, fumbling in her pocket for one of her brown cigarettes. "I've narrowed it down."

"To what?" asked Adine.

"Not telling." Aunt Irene was wearing a sleeveless orange shift printed with a pattern of navy blue cat silhouettes in diagonal lines. Over that she had on a long-sleeved paisley blouse in a myriad of colors, as a smock. She's competing with the wall for attention, Adine thought. Aunt Irene seemed fatter and older to Adine that morning. Maybe because Adine was angry that Aunt Irene got to pick Baby's name. Aunt Irene had three chins, rather than two; she seemed to fill the nursery like a Macy's Thanksgiving Day parade balloon. When Aunt Irene stood in front of the window and sunlight shone behind her, her hair was so wispy that you could see the curve of her head. Adine could tell what her aunt would look like bald—not pleasant. "Baby's name'll be perfect. I promise," Aunt Irene assured. Then, under her breath, barely audible over Bernice and Carla's squabbling and Dot's singing, she added, "I finally want to do *something* right."

But Adine heard her. And for the first time in her life she felt a kind of sadness for her aunt. A brief, sudden sadness that left Adine homesick in the only home she'd ever lived in, surrounded by her entire family.

13

The Lunch Box

The zebra wall had been finished on a Saturday. On Sunday, all the pieces of furniture—dresser, miniature rocking chair, the bookshelf that stored diaper boxes, the old wobbly table used for changing—were painted metallic silver, and a gleaming, new chrome crib was bought at the outlet mall. When the nursery was set up, everything in its proper place, the crib was a silvery cage in the center of a small, square room that pulsed with enough boldness and energy to fill a house. The next day, Monday, all the Vorlobs overslept. Mr. Vorlob was late for work. And the children were late for school.

"Probably because of all the paint fumes," Aunt Irene joked. "We must have breathed them in."

Upon hearing that, Carla started gasping and swooning. She asked to stay home from school.

"Nice try, but no dice," Mrs. Vorlob said, rolling her eyes at Carla. "Don't overdramatize. Your dad moved the alarm clock into the nursery while we painted. He forgot to move it back."

Because they were running late, there wasn't time for Adine's morning routine. Usually she'd wash and dress quickly and run down to the den to watch Willard Scott's weather segment on the "Today" show before breakfast. Sometimes her sisters would join her. Bernice thought that Willard Scott and Aunt Irene would make a good couple. She even called him Uncle Willy. "They'd look great together," Bernice would say. "Just about the same size." After hearing the forecast, Adine would go to the kitchen to eat.

Adine's favorite breakfast was two pieces of white bread (the soft, squishy kind), toasted, with margarine, banana slices, and cinnamon and sugar in between. She'd press the toast together with the heel of her hand. Starting at one corner, she'd nibble all the crusts off first, then take large bites to finish the rest. Mr. Vorlob dubbed them "Queen Adine's Breakfast Dreams." He'd usually have three of them with a tall glass of milk. One was enough for Adine.

But that morning there wasn't time for Willard Scott and breakfast. While the girls dressed themselves, Mrs. Vorlob wrote excuses for them to give to their teachers, and Aunt Irene packed their lunch boxes and lined them up on the kitchen counter. Then Aunt Irene threw on her robe and slippers and ran out to start her car. She revved the engine and waited. Most mornings Adine, Bernice, and Carla walked, but this morning Aunt Irene had offered to drive them to get them to Tyler Elementary as fast as possible. "Hurry!" she called from the street, as the girls poured down the front steps, their unbuttoned jackets flapping at their sides like wings.

They were only fifteen minutes late. Adine, still a bit flustered from rushing, was seated at her desk trying to find her place in her math book when she realized that she had left her lunch box in Aunt Irene's car. But by that time it was already too late. In a matter of seconds, there was a loud banging on the classroom door, followed by Aunt Irene's grand entrance.

Adine's cheeks burned as Aunt Irene shuffled across the front of the room, her fuzzy, hot pink slippers going *swish-swish, swish-swish* on the linoleum. Aunt Irene held Adine's lunch box

out in front of her, and the belt from her bathrobe dragged along the floor behind her. It was
her cat robe, of course—hundreds of black cats
jumping all over it as if they were being shot
out of a popcorn popper. Wispy black feathers
trimmed the sleeves and collar. "Adine Vorlob
forgot this," Aunt Irene told the teacher. "I'm
her Aunt Irene."

Giggles. Snickers. Laughter.

Adine wanted to be somewhere else. Prefer-
ably home, cocooned under the blankets on her
parents' big bed. Or alone in the kitchen carv-
ing her initials in the glassy-smooth top of a
brand-new jar of peanut butter.

As the door closed slowly behind her aunt
like a yawn, Adine flashed her a look that could
break dishes. Then Adine placed her head on
her arms and cried hot tears, clamping her eyes
tightly and drawing her arms closely around
her ears to muffle/all the laughter.

By the time school was over, Adine still felt
miserable. All afternoon, and at dinner, she

avoided looking at and talking to Aunt Irene. "I'm never going back," she told her mother before bed.

"Back where?" Mrs. Vorlob asked.

"School," said Adine. "I'm never going back to school after what happened today."

There were tears and hugs and ear tugging as Adine explained her terrible morning to her mother.

"Can I stay home tomorrow? Please?" said Adine, her eyes widening. "Just one day?"

"Oh, honey, it's usually better to just face things right away."

"Please?"

Mrs. Vorlob thought a moment and sighed. "Okay, I guess. Just this once. Just one day." She brushed Adine's hair aside and placed her hand firmly on Adine's forehead. "Well, you do have a little temperature, you know," she said winking.

14

Rain

There was a sound like drummers playing. And something shadowy and nameless was chasing Adine. Against her will she remained motionless, rooted to the ground with legs of stone. The thing got closer and closer, and then it rumbled and made a frightening noise.

The noise was so loud that Adine woke up.

She had been dreaming. Her room was dark. It was raining. Lightning lit up the room for a second, and Adine held her breath until the following thunderclap shook the windows. Adine ran to the kitchen.

"I hear you've got a fever," said Aunt Irene. She was sitting at the kitchen table in her cat robe and hot pink slippers. Before her was a plate of frozen waffles, toasted (nearly black), cut into tiny squares, and buried with strawberry jam.

Adine nodded. "Where's Mom? Where's everyone else?" she asked, her eyes directed away from Aunt Irene.

"Your dad's at work. Your mother just left— she drove your sisters to school and then she wanted to go grocery shopping. She took Dot and Effie with her. And Baby's sleeping." Aunt Irene pushed a piece of waffle around her plate. "I told your mother I'd watch Dot and Effie, but she said she wanted to take them with her.

She said she felt funny not having at least a couple of kids along."

Adine felt betrayed. By everyone. How could her mother leave her with Aunt Irene after what had happened at school? Especially while it was storming?

Mustering all her courage, Adine walked to the back door—tripping on Deedee and nearly falling—and looked out the window. The sky was a horrible choppy sea, lightning separating it like a crooked grin. Deedee was meowing, doing figure eights around Adine's feet, rubbing against Adine's legs.

Adine wanted her mother. Now.

"If you're sick," Aunt Irene called from the kitchen, "you shouldn't be by that drafty door."

"Oh, be quiet," Adine whispered ever so softly. There was no confusion about how Adine felt about her aunt at this moment.

"Adine—" called Aunt Irene again.

"I'm coming," muttered Adine, her voice

trembling with fear (because of the storm) and anger (because of Aunt Irene). But before she did come, she quietly opened the back door and scooted Deedee outside. Deedee scratched on the door, trying to get back in. Thunder crashed, and Deedee, bewildered, sprinted into the neighbors' bushes. Adine watched until Deedee disappeared. Would she come back? She wasn't an outdoor cat. If she ever did go out, it was on a leash, with Aunt Irene holding on tightly. Adine hadn't thought about what she had done. It had just happened. As if some button inside her had been accidently pushed. But she felt a kind of satisfaction. As if she had gotten even.

The minutes dragged like hours. At intervals, Adine called the weather information recording, using the extension phone in her parents' room. She held down on her lower lip with her teeth while she listened. It was supposed to rain most of the day, clearing late in the afternoon. There was no mention of a tornado, thank goodness. Between calls, Adine passed the time by keeping Baby company in the nursery, picking him up out of his crib and holding him during the thunder and lightning. Baby seemed unafraid, but Adine felt better just touching someone. She pretended she was needed. "It's okay," she told her brother.

Like clockwork, Adine shortly went to her parents' room to call the weather recording again. She picked up the receiver and—instead of a dial tone—heard Aunt Irene talking to one of her friends. Aunt Irene was using the phone in the kitchen. Adine became still as stone.

"I don't know what I'd do without Helen and Roland and the girls. Baby, too," Aunt Irene said. "Those girls are the kids I never had."

Adine's heart did anxious things.

Aunt Irene continued, "I'm fifty-two and what do I have to show for it?" (Sniffle.) "No husband. No children. Just Deedee. Just my precious cat. . . ."

As quietly as possible, Adine hung up the phone. And then, without giving it a second thought, her pajamas still on, Adine ran down the steps, through the living room, out the front door, and into the rain.

15

Storm in a Teacup

"Goodness!" exclaimed Aunt Irene, whirling around with a start as Adine tried to sneak into the kitchen. "Where on earth have you been? I thought you were up in our room. And Deedee—where was *she*?"

"I went to get Deedee," Adine said, choosing her words carefully. "She was outside," she added, dropping Deedee on the wet floor.

Adine was drained and drenched and muddy from running throughout the neighborhood and alleyway behind their house, calling frantically for Deedee—and crying. Her pajamas and hair were dripping, making dirty puddles at her feet. Deedee shook her front paws off—first one then the other, one then the other—until Aunt Irene picked her up and planted noisy kisses all across her face.

When Adine had finally found Deedee, she had been lying by the side of the neighbors' garage, a snug ball huddled in a small shelter formed by some garbage cans. Adine had never liked holding Deedee, so she snatched her up quickly, hoping she wouldn't scratch or bite. It had been Adine's intention to simply get Deedee back into the house and clean herself up without Aunt Irene's noticing a thing.

"You'll catch pneumonia," said Aunt Irene, handing Adine a towel from the pantry. "If you haven't already. Dry off and I'll put water on for some nice, hot tea." Aunt Irene turned her back to Adine and set the teakettle on the stove. "Thank you, Adine," she said.

Deedee was grooming herself now. She stopped for a second and gloated as if she owned the kitchen table (where she sat), not to mention the entire room. When Deedee stretched her legs, her claws popped out of her paws like weapons.

"How did you get out?" Aunt Irene asked Deedee in baby talk. "How did you ever get out?"

Deedee paid no attention. She thrust her leg out like a ballerina and attacked the fur on her flank.

And then, suddenly, as if it had only just sunk in, Aunt Irene said, "My goodness. Thank you again, Adine. Thank you, thank you, thank you. I just couldn't live without Deedee." She shook her head in disbelief, then sighed in relief.

Adine began to shiver. She tugged on her ear and rocked on her heels, thinking. Without warning, she rushed over to Aunt Irene and threw her arms around her. "I *pushed* her out," she squeaked. "Deedee, I mean. I pushed her outside. On purpose," Adine managed to whisper before letting out a sob into Aunt Irene's bathrobe.

After a few minutes of Aunt Irene's saying, "There, there," Adine calmed down enough to whisper, "I'm sorry." Adine tightened her hug for a second before letting go.

"You don't have to say that," Aunt Irene told Adine. "*I'm* sorry." She pulled a wad of tissues out of her sleeve and handed it to Adine. "I hate tears, you know. How about a smile?"

Adine tried her best to accommodate, but her smile was more a forced grin than a genuine smile.

"I'm not going to ask you why you did what you did," Aunt Irene said, gently shoving Deedee off the table, "because I have more than an idea." She hesitated, rubbing her hands together, her eyes misting over. "Your mother told me you were embarrassed yesterday—and I apologize. We were in such a hurry, I just forgot what I had on. How stupid . . ." Her voice trailed off. "Why don't you go take a quick, hot shower and change," she suggested, obviously trying to sound cheerful. She tipped her head away. "I'll fix the tea. It'll be all ready by the time you're back."

The teapot was piping hot; steam rose from its spout like chimney smoke. Adine inhaled deeply as Aunt Irene filled both cups. The tea smelled wonderful. Adine pulled herself closer to the table. She shivered, just thinking about being out alone in the rain. It was only drizzling now, a fine mist hanging in the air like a cold veil over the house. The kitchen was warm, though. Adine settled back into her chair.

Adine watched Aunt Irene spoon sugar and pour two dollops of cream into her teacup. The cups were thin as paper and dainty. Pastel flowers decorated them, inside and out. The rims were tipped in gold.

"Want some?" asked Aunt Irene, gesturing toward the sugar and cream.

Adine nodded.

Aunt Irene passed the sugar bowl and tiny cream pitcher to Adine. "You can make a storm in your teacup," said Aunt Irene.

"What?" replied Adine.

Aunt Irene explained. The tea was the dark sky. The cream formed the clouds. And the sugar—shaken into the cup—was the rain falling.

Adine made a storm in her teacup and swirled it around. She stared at it. The cream churned and exploded. Just like a real storm. Only very small. Finally, Adine stirred it well, the storm disappearing.

Funny, thought Adine, how a storm in a teacup isn't scary at all. So tiny you can fit it into your hand. She giggled at that.

Adine took a big gulp and her throat felt like it was on fire.

"Take sips," Aunt Irene told her.

"I'm afraid of storms," Adine said after a while, into her cup. "Real ones."

"Everyone's afraid of something," said Aunt Irene.

Adine couldn't picture her parents being afraid of anything. Carla or Bernice, either. Maybe, thought Adine, I've got enough fear in me to make up for everyone else in my family. "Are *you* afraid of anything?" Adine asked quietly.

Aunt Irene laughed and shook her head yes. "And I wish it were only storms." She sighed; her face seemed to inflate, then relax.

Adine didn't press for a more specific answer.

For a long time they sat in silence. Between sips, Adine folded her hands on the table before her and wiggled her fingers, weaving them. She felt an urgency rise inside her, knotting her stomach. There was something else Adine wanted to tell Aunt Irene about. The pictures. The pictures that she and Carla and Bernice had drawn. Adine was certain that Aunt Irene had found them. She wanted to apologize. She wasn't sure where to start.

"There were these pictures," Adine began abruptly, curling her toes around the rung of the chair. "In the closet . . . and . . ."

"Hushhh," Aunt Irene murmured, bringing her finger to her lips. She rose from the table and started clearing it off. "It seems to me I did find some crazy scribblings of something or another in the closet one day. I thought it was scrap paper. I tossed it all into the garbage without really looking." Aunt Irene was talking so fast, her words almost ran together. "That's that," she said with finality, clapping her hands once.

Adine guessed that what Aunt Irene had just said wasn't exactly true. But it was exactly what Adine needed to hear.

After putting the cream pitcher in the

refrigerator, Aunt Irene changed the subject. "How about we go check on your brother? I haven't heard a peep out of him all morning."

Aunt Irene picked Baby up and patted the top of his head. Then she carefully handed him to Adine. Adine kissed him on each cheek.

Baby opened his squinty eyes completely and stared at Adine fiercely. His head bobbed like the float on a fishing line, but his eyes remained fixed on his oldest sister.

"I'm thinking of announcing his name tonight," Aunt Irene said, her hand moving like an insect across Baby's crib rail. "After dinner."

Baby blew a bubble. And smiled when it popped.

"Can you keep a secret?" asked Aunt Irene. Adine nodded.

"Baby's name is going to be Zeke," Aunt Irene said in a hushed voice. "But don't tell anyone. No one knows. What do you think of it? Zeke. Nice, huh?"

Adine frowned. *Zeke?*

"You don't like it, do you?" Aunt Irene asked.

Adine shrugged. She remembered a garbage collector they used to have named Zeke. He had brown and yellow teeth, and he always screamed at the neighborhood children when they watched him work in the alley. But, at least Zeke was a better name than Baby. Adine imagined her brother in the fourth grade, carrying a backpack with BABY VORLOB labeled on the strap. She winced. Someone like Gary Wilker would have a field day with a situation like that.

"What name would you choose?" asked Aunt Irene. "If it were up to you."

"I like Zachary. Not Zack for short. Zachary."

"Hmmmm," said Aunt Irene, twisting her mouth. She looked at Adine through her thick glasses, leaning her chin into her hand thoughtfully. "I have a feeling your mother would say a name like that sounds a bit self-important. She's so particular about names. Me—I don't think they matter that much."

Adine did. She thought they mattered a lot.

Aunt Irene continued, as if she had read Adine's mind. "I mean, a name can't make someone nice or pretty or funny. People just are the way they are. Period."

Zeke, thought Adine. It would be hard to get used to.

After gently laying Zeke back in his crib, Adine stood over him until he appeared motionless. Still as a statue. Adine leaned on the rail and listened for a heartbeat. It was there— tiny but constant. Almost strong, when she lightly pressed her ear to his chest and concentrated on listening with all her might.

Adine wondered if Zeke would grow up to hate his name. If he'd grow up to be a garbage collector. She wondered if he would grow up differently if his name were Zachary. If she would be someone else if she had been named

Angelique. Or maybe Aunt Irene was right. Maybe it didn't matter.

From downstairs came the sounds of people returning—doors opening and closing, footsteps on stairs. Mrs. Vorlob was home. Adine blew a kiss to Zeke, and she and Aunt Irene tiptoed out of the nursery. "Remember, don't tell," whispered Aunt Irene.

"I won't."

"You know," Aunt Irene said as they entered the hallway, "I just thought of something. Speaking of names: Adine, Irene—they almost rhyme."

16

The Mobile

The entire family was in the nursery, circling the crib. Aunt Irene stood at the foot of the crib with her hands behind her back. She cleared her throat. "Before I tell you Baby's new name, I want to hang this." She pulled a mobile out from behind her. "I made it," she told them brightly.

It looked handmade. There were six

Styrofoam balls, each painted with black zebra stripes. The stripes coiled around the balls like the whorled lines of a fingerprint. The balls were attached by cord to a wire support. Aunt Irene hung the mobile, and the balls bobbed and spun.

"There's one ball for each of you," Aunt Irene explained. "Adine, Bernice, Carla, Dot, Effie, and . . . Zachary."

Zachary? What about Zeke?

Adine could barely believe it. But she kept hearing the name over and over. Zachary, Zachary, Zachary.

"Now, remember," Aunt Irene said, "none of this Zack-for-short business. His name is Zachary. It's very important to me."

Everyone seemed happy about the name. Even Mrs. Vorlob.

Aunt Irene lit one of her brown cigarettes and blew smoke rings. She leaned against the zebra wall while everyone else greeted her nephew by his new name. Her eyes caught Adine's and sparkled. Aunt Irene winked.

No one seemed to notice as Adine came up to Aunt Irene. Inconspicuously, Adine grabbed her aunt's hand and squeezed it. "Adine, Irene—they *do* almost rhyme," she said smiling.

Adine lingered in the nursery after everyone else had left. With the lamp off, the room was washed in light from the moon. From the window, where Adine stood, the zebra wall was softened. It appeared to be bluish gray and silver, rather than black and white. But it didn't take much imagination to picture it the way it really was.

It occurred to Adine that the zebra wall was a lot like Aunt Irene. Big and bold. From a distance, the edges of the stripes looked sharp, but close up they were uneven and fuzzy in places. Feathery. Each one was different; the stripes seemed to have minds of their own—first curving this way, then tilting that way.

The Mobile

Adine walked to the wall and ran her fingers over some of the stripes. Then she went to the crib. She studied Zachary. He twitched and grimaced in his sleep, as if he were trying to grow right before Adine's eyes.

It was only ten years ago, but Adine couldn't remember what it was like to be so little. Adine wondered what Zachary would be like when *he* was ten. Adine would be twenty then. She could hardly wait. The possibilities were endless.

"Good night, Zachary," Adine whispered. She accidently knocked the mobile as she rose from kissing him. It twirled and turned. Around and around. As if in a dream, the mobile seemed to take off and fall into place against the night sky. Like a small solar system, alive among the stars. Each Styrofoam ball a shiny world all its own.